MAN ON THE MOVE

Otto de Kat

MAN ON THE MOVE

Translated from the Dutch by
Sam Garrett

MACLEHOSE PRESS
QUERCUS · LONDON

First published in Great Britain in 2009 by

MacLehose Press
an imprint of Quercus
21 Bloomsbury Square
London WC1A 2NS

First published as DE INSCHEPER by Uitgeverij G.A. van Oorschot,
Amsterdam, 2004
Copyright © 2004 by Otto de Kat

English Translation Copyright © 2009 by Sam Garrett

A CIP catalogue reference for this book is available
from the British Library

ISBN 978 1 906694 08 1 (HB)

10 9 8 7 6 5 4 3 2 1

Typeset in Minion by Libanus Press Ltd
Printed and bound in Great Britain by Clays Ltd, St Ives plc

MAN ON THE MOVE

1

He leaned against the rail of the *Cape Town*, the ship of his flight. From below, the engines throbbed, he saw the water turn to foam. Untied. On the quay they were waving. In the group that had come to see him off, his father and mother stood at the front. Blocking his view. He had to leave, get away, he wanted to be gone.

The waving became more frantic, its spell unavoidable. He caught his name: "Rob . . . bye!" It was his mother. His father, watching in silence, doffed his hat almost solemnly then snapped it back in place. He meant to wave, but instead stuck his hand into his inside pocket. The small bundle of letters with places he could go, references, people his father knew. He tore them very deliberately in two, not angrily, only relieved. *His* goodbye.

In the cold, hazy January light the shreds went fluttering down. Would his father understand what he was saying? How could he know that those little shreds of paper would float through his father's dreams for ever. That his mother, for the rest of her life, would see the hand that tore the letters. Who can tell what another person thinks and understands.

Two worlds slid apart.

January, 1935. The shore was too distant now to identify details. The skyline of Rotterdam became indistinct, the endless rocking set in. He turned from the rail, strangers walked past on the darkening deck. Cold wind from England. But he was for South Africa, for summer. The old *Cape Town* had made the journey many times; for him it was the first. South Africa was his escape, his chance to become the adventurer he thought he was, the soldier of fortune he had dreamed up. Unrest had housed in him since childhood. Cross-grained, not at ease with the commonplace, never settling for what others seemed to want. He was never the one to follow everyday rules. "Heads down!" he cried to his classmates, then pulled out an air pistol and, through an open window, shot a crow out of the tree in the schoolyard. Just before his final exams, which he would have passed easily, he gave it all up. He lived by impulse, even at an early age no-one could keep him in check. He climbed out of the window of a moving train and arrived at the next station lying on the roof. For no good reason, just because. He bought a motorcycle, drove it all night to see a girl across the country. After exchanging a few words, he turned round and rode back. He collected sweethearts, the Clark Gable of the Rhine. His unrest only grew.

The weeks at sea lulled him to sleep, to indolence, to irksome memory. But as soon as the ship reached a port of call he would roll ashore with the crew. Hunger for where he had never walked before – Lisbon, Casablanca, Dakar; thirst for the stories of the ship. After thirty days it was over. With sea legs now, a hardened stomach and two suitcases, he disembarked in Cape Town. No-one there he knew. The heat took him in its arms, a leaden heat he had never experienced before. The whiteness of the houses blinded him. The customs officers detained him for a long time, endlessly it seemed. Why did he want to come ashore, where did he plan to go? Whom did he know? The letters, damn it, he had torn up the letters. Hostility was in the air of the half-darkened port office with its slow ceiling fan. He persevered. Nothing was going to keep him out of this country. He told them how for years he had dreamed of Africa. No, he could not come in just like that. No, he would have to find a job if he wanted to stay. He was looking to make his life in Johannesburg, he wanted to work in the goldmines. Surely he had not spent weeks at sea only to be sent back, back to the crisis in Europe. Surely he had not spent years longing for a different life only to let this life be shattered in the first immigration office he came across. With his textbook

English and a great deal of charm, he talked his way into the country. Impelled by the officers' words, he set out to find the railway station, bought a ticket to Johannesburg, and was on his way within the hour.

"Well driven, Engineer," he would hear his father say whenever he got off a train and passed the drivers' cabin. His father, who seemed to control the world, big man in little town. His father who tried to rein him in, and against whom his resistance had grown.

Johannesburg, city of gold – fifty years ago nothing but a camp where men with picks and shovels had dug themselves into the ground. Slowly he followed the crowd off the platform and outside, little man in big town.

This was the moment, here he would live, in the wilds, without references, without a community, alone. For as long as the station hall sheltered him, it still seemed possible to turn back. Then he was out on the street, in a riot of noise. Once more the sweltering heat surprised him, as it had in Cape Town. Black people everywhere, blacker than the few he had come across in Holland. Indians, white men in top hats. Manhattan in Africa, he knew the city's nickname, but as he walked there now, looking up, Johannesburg closed in on him. Was that a trap he heard slam shut? The sea suddenly seemed an implausibility, his long journey had come to an abrupt end. His suitcases felt heavy as gold ingots. But he scarcely had a shilling left.

"Hey, Boss, can I help you?" offered a boy of fifteen or so near the entrance to the mine. He turned, looked at him and asked the boy's name.

"Yoshua, Boss."

"O.K., come along, but stay behind me, you won't yet be used to finding your way down there."

Yoshua's brand new boots with their metal caps glinted in the dusky cage that took them underground. Within minutes they had plummeted more than a kilometre and a half.

The first time he himself had gone down the mine he had been perplexed, but not afraid. Disbelief at the lift cage that kept going down and down, for a seeming eternity. It could not be, no-one could dig that deep, it could not be done. Utter darkness, from before the Day of Creation. His mouth went dry, his skin beaded with sweat. It was a reverse birth, like being buried alive. The electric light when he stepped out disoriented him even more. Slowly, half-blinded, he shuffled behind his crew, along galleries, more galleries, around the corner and again more galleries. Into the hairline cracks of the mine, clambering and crawling. Till there was no light left save that of his own lantern. His first eight-hour shift below had made his head spin. The darkness prowled around him, in the distance was the rattling of machines, the thumping of ore cars on their rails, the shouts of fellow miners. Tossed away into a forbidden universe, unravelled, filthy. He had been numbed, just as on his wild escapade through the Dutch night. Electrically up, electrically down, eight hours on, eight hours off, eight hours sleep. His first weeks, his first self-planned days, his unsettling new life.

Into the mine he went, the boy behind him. He sensed Yoshua's confusion, and looking back he saw his cautious movements, the sheen of puzzlement across his boyish face. Calmly and without hesitation he led him to their new night task. They had left the bulbs behind them, the pitmen had spread out, there were not even rails in this narrow corridor. He set his lantern on a rock.

"Where do you live, boy?"

Yoshua answered in short sentences, speaking of his family in a muddle of English and Swazi. Snatches of it were comprehensible, but most of it was not. Fifteen years at ground level, always out on the streets, not much to hope for, the life of a young black kid, proud of the work boots he had been given. His scheme had worked; he had found a white boss to offer him protection and a modest wage.

Yoshua had stayed. He was there every morning, waiting so that they could go into the mine together. And every morning Rob passed him the lantern, cigarettes and some water. The boy belonged to him. The guards at the gates waved them through with a gesture that said: Good going, Dutchman. But he had done nothing, it was the boy who had presented himself, who just turned up. Sent by a foreman as a spare hand. In the weeks and months that followed, a tenuous friendship came into being. Yoshua carried the lighter tools and their water. He pottered around his boss, ran to him whenever his cigarette needed lighting. "*Kunjani*, Boss?" he said each day at the mine entrance, "How is it going?" He taught Yoshua to work the acetylene lamp, and warned him over and over never to drop their matches. Matches were vital, darkness one of their enemies. The mine became their shared adversary, almost strangling them with its innumerable corridors. The treacherous, deadly mine, the lurking beast. Yoshua knew all about beasts. He knew the mountains around Johannesburg, had crossed the fringes of the Kalahari with his father. He had avoided serpents' bites and walked ravines where the sun never shone.

He told his boss that his father travelled all the time, sometimes for more than a year. And his mother worked for white people.

They talked while sitting on a rock, eating their lunch, or taking the cage back up. But in the early morning they were mostly silent, steeling themselves against a day underground. They learned each other's ways, respected each other's silences. And, although he was the master, he always remembered that the boy was more a part of this land than he. His own youth, in a provincial town on a river, was an abyss away from them. What could he tell Yoshua? That he feared having to march along through an orderly existence. His brothers were at college, and no doubt would turn out fine. His father ruled the town. And his mother, his dear, beloved mother? He did not want to think about her. His life in South Africa could not support the idea of her, he could not let her get to him, she was his weak spot. The spot Yoshua always knew just how to find.

"My mother, Boss, she wakes me up in the morning, and every day she asks me to please be careful. She's afraid of the mine. But we're not, are we Boss?" Yoshua looked up at him as he stepped out of the cage.

"We're not, boy."

The boy held up the cigarettes. The match burned bright, and with their hands cupped around it and their heads bowed together they cast huge silhouettes. A shadowy place of groping your way forward. The rough, cavernous world that shook with explosions. Yoshua's boots glinted each time he lifted the lantern. Yoshua's mother was worried, it seemed, and of course so was his own. He had not written much since living in Johannesburg. His work as a gold coolie did not allow much time, and when it did he preferred the greyhound track at Wembley. Thousands of gamblers were there each Wednesday evening, the races were the highlight of the week. In his naivety he had once asked Yoshua to come with him. The boy had looked at him blankly, and had not even replied.

His bond with the boy grew. He watched him go at the end of each day when they parted at the gate. Yoshua seemed immune to fatigue. He walked home each evening with a fresh bounce in his step, skipping almost. Sometimes he wished he could go along into the world of Yoshua, to shake his mother's hand and tell her how well her son found his way through the mine, how he moved down the galleries, cautious as a hunter after a large prey. But that never happened.

"Watch out, Boss!"

Their corridor had been shored up only recently. The implosion of their working area sucked his breath away even as he jumped aside. The sharp warning cry was suspended in the air in the silence that followed, and he could not tell whether the boy's shout had come before or after the cave-in. Then he heard the moans. He called, found his lantern, cast about him, found Yoshua. In the light he saw him lying, the matches clenched in his hand. His head twisted unnaturally, arms wide, a boulder straight across his back. He opened his eyes. "*Kunjani*, Boss?" he asked, intensely worried. But death came sooner than the words that should have reassured Yoshua.

At the gates the guards nodded as he walked beside the stretcher. "Bad luck, Dutchman." The mine worked on. Yoshua's mother could only take the morning off for the funeral. His father was still away.

During the long marches from Ban Pong to the River

9

Kwai, he would think again and again of those eyes, and of that question too kind for words.

Dog races on Wednesday nights were alternated with reading the newspapers, usually in the Star Beer Hall on Rissik Street. The city began to absorb him. Walking with the crowd to the stadium or stepping into the local restaurant where he ate each night, he seemed a part of it all. What drove him, though, was the thought of being independent, of being himself, finally. The rooms he rented were bare. At home every table and lampshade had a history, almost none of it had been bought. Here nothing had been handed down, no ancestors on the walls; china and silver sparkled only in his memory. But he made the disconcerting discovery that objects had a meaning. Sometimes he would draw what he had left behind. Dutch objects he never saw any more. His childhood room in Honk, the stately house with the pillars, the broad steps and the ivy up to his window. Casual drawings scribbled in idle hours, then promptly thrown away. First he had wanted to suppress all thought of the people living in that distant house, but then the objects too were buried. And so his rooms remained Spartan. Holland was not admitted; it would undermine the sense of adventure.

As a soldier of fortune was how he liked to think of himself. But when the telegram giving news of his father's death lay on the table, it was very hard not to drop everything and say goodbye to it all. Yet his reluctance to go there, to the sombre ceremony, the sombre land, won out. Let the dead bury the dead. He worried that his mother would ask him to stay. He did not want to lose himself again. And so he did not go. He left his old life for what it was, and let his father's death be.

Later in Thailand, along the tracks, he pictured his father's grave, an image as hard to shake as the countless jungle flies on his skin.

The raw army of the miners was the best possible training. Day and night turned inside out, cold and heat thrumming against his body. He clenched his teeth to pain, his muscles doubled. Gold-digger in a self-chosen free-dom, regardless of what he had been or should become. One year, two years, five – submerged, prowling, timeless, solitary.

The speed with which Johannesburg grew astounded him and everyone else. The provincial town on the Dutch river shrank and faded. The Africans built like mad. Girders to the heavens, twenty storeys and more, flats and department stores. The land buzzed as never before with politics and parties and extortionate prosperity. South Africa was borne up on waves of expectation. Gold was still a magic word, a language the whole world understood. Walking the streets, he imagined a tickertape parade, cabriolets and drum and pipe bands in a storm of tumbling paper.

A lifetime away, in Manila, he would be welcomed like that, all skin and bone, with hundreds of others, as the crowds cheered like madmen.

2

Dete ike, dete ike, dete ike! – out, out, out! – always the
same razor-sharp command in otherwise unintelligible
Japanese. Anyone who did not fall or jump was beaten out.
Twenty-five men to a car, forty boxcars, a constant echo
of orders. Accustomed as he was to rapid change from
darkness to light, he saw at once the ravages the train
journey had wrought. Five days and nights in rattling
tumult between the zinc walls of a boxcar. The drills in the
mine had made less noise. Five days and nights of thirst
and dust and locomotive fumes. The first unsteady steps,
the first pain. The disbelief at finding himself on solid
ground, and the sense of something terrible nearing.

Crammed in at Singapore, vomited out in Ban Pong.
Despicable Europeans who had not fought to the death.
The Japanese were not fond of survivors. Thailand, April,
1943. He had imagined his thirtieth birthday differently.
They would march to the Kwai, two hundred and fifty

kilometres through crushing heat and torrential rain. A handful of rice, filthy water, from hunger-hole to malaria camp.

"Guus!" he cried, "Guus!"

His friend had to be a few cars down. He saw him coming, with amazed little steps as though he had just invented walking. "Guus, we must stay close, whatever happens." And stay close they did. They had met at Bandung one year earlier. His friendship with Guus would never let him go. Would enlighten, levitate and haunt him. Later, into the pointless time, into a dark future, Guus, damned, doomed Guus. A shadow he became, an invisible gazelle, a strange mirror in which he thought to find himself. Guus, in everything his equal, in everything his master. The man he recognized, who confronted him with his flight and his ramshackle ideals.

The Japs had won the war, thousands of prisoners herded together. During roll calls at their camp, Guus had always appeared in the row in front of him. The back of his head grew familiar, his parting down the middle, his slender, wiry figure. Whenever and wherever they could, they sought each other's company. Guus' past was not far removed from his own: shipped out to the Indies as a volunteer, just like he. Volunteers: a remarkable term for those who wander into a snare set by others. The fatherland, what was left of it – the Indies, that is – had to be defended, protected; it was theirs. The delicate web of

14

reasons why, woven by nobody and by everyone. The great unsung human decoys for misfortune. They went. Guus from England, where he had worked for a Dutch concern. He himself from South Africa, where he had worked to prove himself different from his brothers, more independent, more mature. He had boarded the *Tegelberg* for Java with a band of Dutchmen, on their way, of their own free will, to the unthinkable. The last days on shore he had spent in a Durban hotel. The world there was clear as crystal. His decision to sign up had raised in him a featherlight recklessness. The girl he had spent those days with was excitingly exotic. Spontaneously, she said she wanted to marry him there and then. He left even before he got to know her properly. Maybe he had signed up to shake her off, to spare her. Marriage was something for his brothers. He went to find the war, alibi of the orphaned. He left. The ship zigzagged out of the harbour, mimicking the course of his life, he thought, looking back to the African coast.

The march to the Kwai began and ended in the dark. At night they dragged themselves down elephant paths through a leeching jungle. During the day they slept fitfully, swarmed upon by mosquitoes, hollow with hunger. Already at Bandung he and Guus had devised a survival strategy. They began to unravel each other's lives and pasts, threaded together the beads of stories. Related countless details that struck them during the day. They collected little incidents, swapped absurdities, observed minimal shifts in the tone of the camp. The number of lashes meted out, the distance between forehead and ground when bowing to the Japanese sergeant. They counted the grains of rice in their scoop of rations, how long the sun shone on their sleeping mats, the sores on their comrades' feet. Anything was allowed, every new discovery was checked and weighed. Their life depended, it seemed, on a stream of concoctions and memories. They practised looking, saw almost immediately when the Japs changed their plans, were readying for an execution, devised new punishments. Every move the Jap made was stored in them. They synchronized their daily rhythms, seldom lost sight of each other. Instinct, front and back covered, an armoured eye in the face of blistering violence.

The jungle had the hospitality of a bloodsucker. A sickening curtain of trees and bushes seemed to offer escape, yet whoever fled was lost. During night marches of twenty, twenty-five kilometres through the tumult of age-old forests, men fell by every wayside. Too tired, too sick to go on. Numbed, utterly indifferent to death. He and Guus beat time with everything they had taught themselves at Bandung. To not have to think about the next day, or the next night. Ten days the knockout race lasted. They had left with a thousand, arrived at the Kwai with scarcely seven hundred, three hundred of whom could not lift a finger. Sometimes he hallucinated with fatigue. Little

Yoshua bending over him with a pack of cigarettes. Sometimes, seeing a man who had fallen beside the stumbling cavalcade, he would mumble "*Kunjani*, Boss?"

The monsoons were probably the worst. The fatal downpours that flogged their ribs. Sleeping in a puddle of rainwater, rising from a bed of mud. Wetness was next of kin to illness, swamp the father of malaria.

The River Kwai, soft-yellow, almost brown moving water. The camp thrown up on its banks would be the casino of their lives in the months to come. The chances of getting out alive they put at 40 per cent. Three hundred men dead on the journey, three hundred ill. How soon would the sick die, and when would the rest become ill? It was roulette. The croupiers raked in the winnings. The field in which the dead were buried spread to the edge of the forest.

Roll call, before work, after work. Sometimes they stood for hours, most often after work. Heads counted and counted again. Screaming when the numbers did not tally. Recount. Their world stretched from the soles of their feet to their backs, through the pain in between. They were in Thailand, building a railway to Burma, hundreds of kilometres along the river. Building and sabotaging, two steps forward, one step back. He and Guus were in the hacking crew. They used handmade picks to hack through rock, so that an imaginary train could pass. The train pursued them. Every punishment, every speech, every extra hour of work, the Jap was obsessed with the train. And therefore so were they. Their train grew to grotesque proportions. They fantasized about its length, the number of cars, the colour of the upholstery. Or would it only be freight cars, with tanks, oil, weapons? In their minds thousands of them began to roll, drawing out the war. The emperor would pass, waving, straight through the jungle. The Japs would bow, they would bow double. The emperor was the watchword; everything happened in his accursed name. The emperor on his bastard island far away, nodded and bowed to from the jungle grass of Thailand. Famished, damn near dead, befuddled by malaria, hollowed out by dysentery, shattered by cholera: those that are hacking salute you.

They hacked. In the morning they walked in single file to where they had left off the night before. With picks over their shoulders heavy as lead, heavier every day. And without shoes. In a way, that made them feel strangely humiliated. Having no shoes made them helpless, in arrears beside the high-booted Jap.

Roll call, a case for punishment, someone caught outside the camp and accused of running away. He stood no more than five sleepers from the runaway. To attention, all night. The condemned man was on his knees, his head bowed. He heard the night forest, the shrieking of monkeys and unknown birds, there was hissing and whispering and crackling. Men fell over left and right and were beaten to their feet, or dragged off. In his mind he was playing chess with Guus. The king was the emperor, the castle was carved of bamboo, the queen had gone to England. It all spun together. Half sleep, half night, half life, half human. When the sun came up the Jap blindfolded the kneeling man. So he did not see the sword come near, did not hear it strike.

"*Kunjani*, Boss?"

He was ordered to drag away the body, along with two other ghosts, confused after standing in numb silence. Behind them, roll call came to an end and the working day began. They brought the dead man to the burying field, grey in the early morning, and improvised a wooden cross. Blood on their feet.

Days and nights like this. He and Guus refused to succumb. Stubborn and drugged by the sun, they marched behind the Jap. Through Thailand, until close to the Three Pagodas Pass. Their survival strategies were wearing thin. Their eyes saw nothing new. Every fresh discovery became a threat, every surprise eating away at their stamina. If there was more than standing, hacking, walking and sleeping, they did not want to know. The train was their obsession, the railway their anchor, the Jap their demon. They lived like tortoises, withdrawing at any moment beneath their protective domes. They believed that this way they did not see, feel, hope. They endured the dead bodies, the atrocities, their total powerlessness. He and

Guus. Or rather: Guus. And he. Each for their own, and the emperor for all. Their twofoldness was temporarily broken. What first had been their strength now became their weakness, although the unspoken bond remained – for when it was badly needed.

Death without end, time without meaning. After the monsoons, the wind. By day an inescapable sun shimmered, the nights were freezing cold. And the day came when the very last rocks were hacked out, the very last sleepers laid. The train would roll, the prisoners would be cast aside. The work was done, the emperor could be pleased with his army of crushed Europeans, trash of his realm.

As in Bandung, the waiting began. Until somewhere a clerk passed down the orders from above: *Disband camps on the Kwai, transport prisoners to the fatherland.* Destination Japan then, the infernal island, the distant pit of evil. They walked back the way they had come. But more despondent now, serfs who believed in nothing any more, displaced and re-displaced. Afoot or carried off in trains, even weaker, more apathetic, less useful to the Jap than before.

They were embarked at Singapore. He found Guus in the hold of the *Bungu Maru*. They had not seen each other since their return journey from the inlands of Thailand. The camps around the harbour were overcrowded, those who had survived the railway were packed into them without any system. But the bureaucrats were regaining ground and assigned adequate troops. Course set for Kyushu, the large, southernmost Japanese island. He thought of the *Cape Town* and the *Tegelberg*, the ships he had known, one bound for freedom, the other steaming towards defeat. And this *Bungu Maru*, no doubt heading for the end. Descending steep ladders into the guts of the troop carrier, he saw him. Skinny, still wearing his parting through the middle of virtually snow-white hair.

"Guus!"

They hugged briefly, with almost no visible emotion, as they hurried to find a place. They settled next to a ladder, nowhere to lie down. Guus had insisted on a space near an escape to the upper deck. He had heard the rumours of torpedoed Japanese transport ships, laden with prisoners of war. The Americans and the Brits hunted down every boat.

And indeed their veering course proved no salvation. A shattering blast brought the sea in immediately. Amidst the immeasurable chaos they were onto the ladder in a few steps. There was a fight above their heads. Two bodies came flailing downwards, the Jap had kicked them off the ladder. But they did not have to wait for long. The ship was screaming and began to gain water. He would never forget the moment Guus jumped. Thirty seconds perhaps before he himself pushed off the rail and smacked onto the water beside a raft. The sea was hard as rock and he screamed with pain. Clutching the life raft, he shouted Guus' name. But in the throng of swimmers all around, he did not discover him. He shouted until at last he had no voice.

Wind straight from Siberia roared across Nagasaki Bay. Winter at its fiercest, 30° below. Kawanami Wharf, where he pottered about, lay beneath a pack of hardened snow. The dirt-coloured hulls of unfinished ships made the desolation complete. He lived as if by clockwork. The cold seized you and could not be escaped. The long coat over his tropical kit only just kept him from freezing, but it felt as though there were ice in his head. Everything slowed, his hands had trouble holding anything, any movement seemed a coincidence. The ship he worked on every day was at the dock site, open on every side, a carcass of bolts and sheet metal. Still, in the belly of the ship he could shelter from the wind. His blood ran a bit faster there, his head thawed out, but there was little life in it. The past was a dark, shapeless sludge. The future was unthinkable, required courage and hope. Both were hibernating. Only the moment mattered.

He folded his fingers one at a time around the mallet handle. He paused between each blow, waiting for the tingling to end. By day, darkness still hung along the scaffolding he worked upon. Temperatures were at an all-time low, even the Jap hardly moved. Despair took hold of him. The years of heat and illness, the years of mines and railway, the years of utter barbarity pressed down on him. Despair for his friend, slender Guus, who had jumped into the sea and vanished. He refused to believe that he had drowned. The scene repeated itself endlessly before his eyes. He replayed the scene, over and over. There was nothing to show that death had taken him down. His leap had been determined, assured, exemplary. His arms almost nonchalantly at his sides, as if it were a game at the pool. A kind of gracefulness, elegant, his white hair recognizable to the last. "See you in the sea, Rob!" he had called. An absurdly level-headed cry amidst all the panic. What had gone wrong? The sea was not rough, where had he swum? Who had pulled him out? He had not found Guus when he was hoisted aboard a Japanese freighter later on. He knew that other ships too had taken on survivors, and he imagined that Guus had been rescued. But then rescued only meant rescued for the moment, a stay of execution. They were kept alive like gladiators, fresh labour awaited them in the land of the rising sun.

From the rim of the iron scaffolding he looked down, his grip on the hammer listless and ever looser. Snow in the bottom of the ship and a dull pounding around him. Men shuffled here and there aimlessly. His lost years. He could not permit himself to think of it, yet it happened. He could no longer manage what he had been so good at with Guus, losing himself in the moment. Guus with his fine-spun talent for only allowing the past to come in when feasible and when needed. His old life. That enormous, shadowy reservoir which he had poured in concrete, sunken fatherland, stowed away. Ice shoring up the dyke of his memory. It had been past midnight. He had rolled his motorcycle noiselessly out of the garage, kicking it into life in the next street. The February night was cold as stone, and at eighty, ninety kilometres an hour the air beneath his jacket froze. He drove without stopping, the wind carving at his cheeks and neck. The route through the polders and open fields took hours, and only at first light did he see the house on which all his thoughts were focused. Embracing the girl who lived there had thrown his whole life into turmoil. He wanted to see her again and convince her to go with him – where to, he did not know, he had not planned. A few days on the bike together, away and back, something like that. She held him off, carefully but determinedly, astonished to see him there so early. She refused to hold him the way she had done so passionately the week before. "You have to put that behind you, Rob. It was a moment, don't cling to it, I don't want to be pinned down." He heard what she said and wheeled his motorcycle around. There rose a chill within him that had nothing to do with the winter air. Riding back with the rising sun behind him felt like racing into a funnel, a snare. By ten he was home. His mother looked worried, his father said nothing. He had expected fury. In the end his father only asked: What was your average speed? No, shorter even: "Average speed?"

The hammer fell from his grasp, the roaring in his head grew louder. He was faint from lack of food, and cold. He had to stay on his feet, he had to extinguish the grip of the past. "Hey, you!" a guard bellowed, pointing at him. "Come down immediately." That probably saved him. The Jap supposed he had been sabotaging the work, and put him on the detail that would go back to the barracks last. It surely saved him. He sealed off his memories, airtight again. Hammered until late in the evening.

The months crumbled. Strangely enough, in his camp the dying had almost come to an end. As if those who had held out until they reached Japan were immune to death. It could go on for an eternity, they had plumbed the depths of their reserves, and in that arid place the very least sufficed. Of the five ships they had worked on, not one had yet been launched. After the winter the bombardments began, and the wharf filled up and emptied, emptied and filled up. He could hear the air-raid sirens echo across the bay. There was no getting away from it now: the war would end. Among themselves they spoke of "liberation" as though it meant something. Liberation was a word out of a magazine, a concept devised to give people a happier look in their eyes. He said the word and was almost ashamed. Regardless of the ending, they would never be free again. Even summer came, with colours that were almost unbearable. Cloudless skies, stars at night, Japan everywhere. Nippon, blood-red cannonball out of a field of magnesium white.

The pamphlets drifted down, a message from Mars: *Don't worry, we'll come.* 9 August, 1945. He had seen the big bombers more often these past few weeks. He had stopped looking up to their growling high above the ship-yard. Did not watch one windy morning when two spotter planes circled Nagasaki and disappeared again. Nor when the B-29 approached at eleven that day. The shipyard was a long way from the city, he felt no threat. *Don't worry, we'll come* – and they had. The small parachute dancing behind the plane, falling to the ground like a vast, white leaf. At 11.02, crowds of people must have watched the parachute. Not him. He was loosening a line of bolts one by one that he had tightened the day before. A game. Penelope unravelling by night the thread that she had spun by day. A parachute with a blistering bomb, the slow germ of all destruction. The Apocalypse perhaps. Total bedazzlement in any case, waves of pure white light, an open-air laboratory. Within moments the landscape was pulverized. The concussion bounced across the bay and in the yard all things wooden were flung to the ground.

He was pushed flat against the hull of his ship and heard the chthonic roar of an unearthly storm. In the brief silence that followed, he peered out. Far across the hills by the city a black column rose, a slow *fata Morgana*. He was overwhelmed by a deep reluctance to watch. He wanted desperately to find his nuts and bolts, and continue his work. He sensed the coming of a great catastrophe.

"*Haiwa arimasu* – Peace has come." The Jap was in shock, incredulous, the echo of a command still in his words. The men stood around him and stared. No-one spoke. The guards seemed smaller than they had been, their faces unreadable as always. The void between the prisoners and guards cautiously filled with sound, talking began, someone cried out, shouts, swelling noise. More planes approached, maddeningly slow. Waving, cheering. *Haiwa arimasu.* The barrack doors stood open, the gates to the yard were unguarded. The feeling of abandonment, the emptiness of freedom. Everything was open, and at the same time impossibly out of reach. Peace. Hardly anyone left the camp, they waited. Where the city of Nagasaki had been was only a crouching life – those who went there went to stoop, to dig. An immense scar. During the first days after the bomb they had been sent in small crews to help out. There had been something holy about the blasted city, a god had run amok there. The place was beyond help.

"Hi, boys, we'll get you out of here" – the first words of genuine liberation American. He watched them arrive in jeeps and heavy trucks, arms slung over the door, cigarettes dangling from their lips. Smoking, eating, activities from before time began, never unlearned. More than a thousand prisoners were in his camp, he knew a few of them, superficially. Now that they were leaving he felt, beneath the surface, the struggle they had put up for years. He would never be free of all those hundreds of skinny men. They had stood back-to-back, avoiding each other's eyes, to survive. Eyes were the only chink in the armour. The sudden looks, exchanged as they left, none of them would forget. Chained by the all-present Jap, entangled in an inexplicable story.

Guus, where would Guus be? Secretly he expected him to hop out of a jeep, as casually as he had sprung into the sea. But it did not happen. They climbed onto the trucks, their bodies protesting against America, nauseous from chocolate and tobacco. Could he really be feeling nostalgia at this leaving? Silent, gazing at the shipyard in the distance, they drove to the harbour. The grim barracks lay abandoned in the warm August day.

Arms around his neck, shivers at the sight of a woman so close. Manila. They were welcomed with music and by American girls who kissed you and held your hands up high and sprinkled confetti on your head. Photographers, drum bands, jeeps full of men from his camp. Straight through a chaotic city built on bomb craters. On Rizal Avenue they left the vehicles and walked a line of cheap bars with all kinds of music, cinemas, restaurants, brothels. No-one asked them to pay. POWs were guests of honour everywhere. Evenings, whole nights in bars and dance halls. Fights and drunkenness, singing and eating. He who laughs loudest is most troubled. Madness in the uniform of the victor. He walked around in a British shirt and American trousers, an Australian army hat on his head, a pair of Japanese officer's boots. A soldier's carnival, thumbing his nose at the years of deprivation. But after a few weeks the fog lifted, and their hosts' interest in the prisoners waned. The Filipinos avoided them, the British and American women had gone home. There was one he had been with all the time. She was gone too. Gone home – the meaning of that word he chose to ignore.

The transports started again. First Batavia. Then on to Singapore, Suez, Durban? Would he go back as he had come?

December in Batavia, like a Western. Everyone carried guns, everyone fired, aiming carefully. There were Indonesian snipers in the trees, pretty good targets themselves. December, 1945. It was only safe to go out in a group, Tommy guns loaded. The menace became almost intolerable, despite the lingering, post-Nagasaki trance. On this stage of his journey he would have to choose his allies every day. He refused to die from a bullet from the local Sukarno militia. The air simmered with violence, the city reeked of hatred and vengeance. A white skin was the least effective camouflage. Respect was reserved exclusively for Sten guns and hand grenades. Sometimes he went to one of the suburbs. It seemed there was less tension there. He was wrong. A woman was dragged off her bicycle before his eyes, her assailants appearing from nowhere. They hacked at her with knives, tore off her clothes. The shots he fired came too late, although a few of them did not get up again.

The surreal heat, the seeming calm after the lightning ambush on the white girl. When some soldiers turned up, he walked away. He had been unable to save her, had been too far off, too slow. He began to believe that the camp had been safer than it was here in liberated Batavia. He wanted to leave, to forget that murdered woman as soon as possible, and this city, this sponge of anger, too. He needed to go home, but which home. He could not bring himself to decide on Holland. If he were to go and live there again, everything would have been in vain.

To go back or not. He mulled it over again, watching as the *Oranje* bore down on the quay. The shuttle between Holland and the Indies. Suez, March 1946. He had left Batavia aboard the *Alcantara*, to be taken to the Red Sea. The Asian islands were behind him at last. The Japs, the Indonesians, hysterical idiots with machetes, all to be banned from his memory. The war was over, he would make up for the years he had lost, wipe them out, put them behind him. The cowardly years of slave labour and kowtowing. The years of self-preservation, waiting in the shadow. A shadow life was what he had lived and even that shadow he was afraid to look at. Be invisible, don't stand out, creep out from your shell only when it's safe. Avoid snares, live like a black cat under the cover of darkness, crouch. The years of want, all five of them, everything within him burned up, hollowed out, evaporated. The *Oranje* manoeuvred skilfully into its moorings. The late light of day fell on the ship full of Dutch families bound for an unknown fatherland. The ship did not seem very cheerful, it was unnaturally quiet on board. He stood on the deck of the *Alcantara* and knew he would have to decide. Tomorrow the *Oranje* would set sail for Holland. In one week the *Felix Roussel* would call at Suez, on its way to South Africa. To go with the *Oranje* was tempting. A gangplank away from his mother and his brothers. He could surprise them. Or embarrass them. Aboard the *Oranje* to the land of his father, the land of the references, the conventional line. The provincial town with his parental home would no longer be there. He had grown out of everything he had once fled from. There was no longing left; the more he thought of Holland, the colder it left him. And he wanted to avoid his mother's old age, fearful of being disarmed. No, not the *Oranje*. He had become too much of a stranger. This was as close as he would come, perhaps, to anyone. He liked to maintain his ability to observe sharply from afar, from behind barricades of his own creating. The Jap had helped him there. He had entrenched himself in his exile. To be everywhere, but nowhere at home. The ship's gentle rocking beneath his feet was a blessing. Evening drew in above the harbour. He knew no-one in Suez. But that did not bother him for a moment. From aboard the *Oranje* he now heard some music, and people singing for someone's birthday. Nothing wild, but a few cheers slipped out. Foolish sentimentality to be affected by that. He listened intently as the words climbed into the Egyptian night. The sheer banality of the song: *long, long shall he live*. What a ludicrous thing to wish anyone. How long had it been since he had been able to sing happy birthday? Camp life had been full of uncelebrated birthdays. You did not mention it, you would sooner put it right out of your mind. But gradually normality crept back. People wished each other a long life again, put garlands on your chair, serenaded you. Who started it? How did normality recover its reign? How to escape those old habits? Impossible.

The singing aboard the *Oranje* did not last long, but just long enough to unnerve him. The intimacy of the Suez evening clashed with the prospect of peace. He was aware of an emptiness; the war was over, his comrades gone to the four winds. Out of sight, out of reach. The peace had broken all bonds, all the roads were open. Every one of them went, some together, some in groups, some alone. Home to wives, children, divorce, another fate.

Waves from the Red Sea reached the quay in Suez harbour at last, to rock the *Alcantara*. They rocked him too, but not to sleep. The forbidden times came back like a boomerang in slow motion. Holland, his father dead, his brothers, his mother. Always his mother. Whom he could count on to celebrate his birthday ten days from now. She would, he knew. 26 March, now she and he could safely think of the day. Would she also be thinking of that other 26 March, so many years ago? It had marked the break with his father, almost beyond repair. There was snow in the streets that day, unusually for the time of year. The table in the big room had been set with family linen, family silver, family china, he remembered ruefully. All of a sudden he had pointed at his father's left eye, an eye made of glass.

"So how many Acehnese did you murder before they shot you down?" he had asked from his festooned chair. He knew the stories his father told, and the stories told about his father, the retired Royal Dutch East Indian Army officer. Stories that had seemed so exciting. About forays in Aceh, helping the people there, punitive expeditions against extremists. He had admired his father extravagantly. His question went against the grain of that admiration. It had seized him, and he blurted it out. Silence had fallen on the table, as before an execution. But no shot was fired. His father seemed caught unawares. His short, awe-inspiring father was speechless. Helpless in the face of a question that was an accusation.

"That's right, I killed fellows who had just finished

slaughtering women and children. You call that murder, I don't. When you're old enough to know about fighting and falling, we'll talk again. But I doubt that time will ever come."

That was the end of the birthday cheer. It had been his last year at home, the last time he had seen Dutch snow, his plan to leave already in place. Fighting and falling – if only his father knew. The irony of an unsuspected life, that he too would be taken into the army of the Indies, father and son in the same uniform, unimaginable on his birthday then. He had his own dead now, three men lying beside that girl in Batavia. His father's glass eye, the fortune teller's crystal ball. History had repeated itself, fate had been duplicated, a dead man upon a dead man. A murder for a murder? He was reluctant to think in such terms now.

The *Alcantara* was moored side by side with the *Oranje*, but he was still a continent away. Seven months had passed since the liberation. The American jeeps had rolled into Japan like phantoms from a world beyond apprehension. They had been swept up, kidnapped out of their measly, calcified lives. Their survival instincts rudely breached. He had grasped the edge of the jeep as he had the raft at sea. Disbelief more than joy. With a mettle born of desperation they had driven out of the camp, the bandit island, the doomed empire, heads bowed. With their heads bowed, for God's sake.

The night in Suez revived the flow of memories. The last months had passed as though under narcosis. It rolled by him, a caravan of events, parade after parade, with women and parties and recklessness. His photograph had been in *Life*, taken at the moment he went ashore at Manila. The photographer shouted something that made him look up. In the background the aircraft carrier on which the Americans had spirited them away from Japan. Around him the surging crowd. "You're the first ones!" the man had said, as though it had been some sort of competition. Looking at the picture, he could never believe it was him. The crew-cut hair, the gaunt face, his ashen skin. In his own eyes he could read the irrecoverable years. His was one of many pictures in the magazine, photographers in action everywhere. The latest fashions in New York, an article about a banker, an interview with a film star, a shower of diversions for the reader. Life goes on, frontlines shift, the world is a news machine. He would turn the pages of the magazine, to see his own face appear among so many others. On the same photograph was the girl who would spontaneously kiss him a few seconds later, and with whom he had wandered through the city for days. He had told this complete stranger about his years in the camps. She listened like no-one had before. Perhaps not even his mother. He talked, he forced himself to account for those terrible, all-devouring years. He was accountable because he was alive and because so many others were not. He struggled with the words, afraid of driving her away, terrified of tumbling into the abyss that he himself had summoned. He toppled from one memory to the next. The fever of telling made him almost literally ill. His emotions, suppressed for so long, could barely survive someone who merely listened. She heard him, asked nothing, held him tight. They roamed Rizal Avenue together, endless hours in cafés and restaurants. They danced, were taken in tow by other POWs, and only slept when morning was well underway. An ebb and flow of stories and an unthinking submersion in liberation parties. Manila was both the drunken binge and the detoxification. The nightmare might have been over, but there was still no dream. Time and again he came back to the river, the yellowish-brown one. Like a dirty, slow adder slithering through the jungle, shaping the course of his thoughts. He tried to find images the woman beside him would understand. There were so many gaps in his memory, he was ashamed of how little he remembered, or wanted to remember. The senseless fight to the finish, the floggings, the executions. He did not touch upon his bond with Guus; he avoided the loss. There were moments, with the girl so close, when his estrangement disappeared. She made him feel that he could take hold of his life once more, belong again some day. The unforgettable nights in Manila, the suspension of time, the wild dancing that broke like a storm over the mountains. Of course it could not last. She would go back to England, and he would be shipped through to Batavia and on. When he walked her to her ship he said nothing, could only look at her. The green of her eyes. After everything he had told her, he simply stood there, speechless. Their parting kindled a sorrow without tears. He had turned around, aware once more of the loneliness he had contracted somewhere, recognizing it. There was something fathomless inside him, a void, an echo, the sound of a motorcycle turning around.

Children were scampering across the deck of the *Oranje*, now he could hear laughter and shouting. A few of them waved to him, their faces just above the gunwale. He waved back, relieved not to be travelling with them. More of them came forward and waved, a whole crowd of children, thrilled to see someone react. It brought him back to Suez, back from the war, and he waved again and again. A lifetime he had spent on board ships, it seemed, waving, leaving, arriving, sinking. A string of ports, but he settled in none of them. He had grown to love it nonetheless; setting sail had become second nature. Oil and water, gulls and quays – the cities were different, but smells and sounds the same everywhere. A week from now the *Felix Roussel* would take him to Durban, South Africa.

The days in Suez sealed his musings. The heat was extraordinary, even Thailand could not match that. He felt looser and lighter than ever.

"Don't be afraid, jump!" a young British navy officer called out. The motorboat did not lie far below the quay, and of course he was not afraid. He jumped resolutely and gave the boat a good rocking. The Englishman had not been expecting him to be so quick and barely kept his balance. Then he leaned on the throttle, full speed ahead. He had no idea where they were going, there was no plan. He sat at the prow, the water spurting past him. Their speed was bewitching. They frolicked past cargo liners coming in from the Red Sea towards the Canal. Graceful and wild, their boat shot past clumsy, hooting freighters. Foam whipped up around them on the bright blue water. The wind, the roar of the motor, he sank into a languor, a state in which all feeling, all desire was extinguished. A fragile, soft and timeless dimension, like days from a distant youth. He sat there at the prow, monk-like, immersed in nothing.

The Englishman at the rudder sang – snatches reached his ears and intensified his detachment. Buddha was not far away. Escaped from the river, the roll call, the bomb. Confused, confounded and here at last, aboard a dancing speedboat: gleeful to the marrow. They chased on and on, mile after mile, in broad arcs. The shoreline shimmered in the sun, the heat palpable even on the water and in the wind. He was not thinking with his brain, he was porous, all skin. Now he was the infatuated vagabond he had once wanted to be. What no-one understood in Holland: his kicking against the inevitable, against a life in shackles. That was what he had emigrated from. He wanted to draft his days at his own drawing table. Days spent down mineshafts and under duress, true. All drafted, drawn by his own hand? The grand illusion. Freedom is a pretty dress on a bulging body, heedless of the looks from all sides. A typical Guus jibe at his chronic ideal. At Camp Bandung especially they still had energy and time enough to put each other to the test. Bandung Oasis, a cluster of villas in the Javanese hills, where wealthy Dutch and Chinese traders built their country homes.

The "nothingness" at the speeding prow gave way to thought in the end. The helmsman slowed, shaking him from his daze. At the quayside he thanked the officer with a curt salute. But once ashore his steps were shaky, a dizziness he could not place. Was it the waves, the thrill of the ride, the old longing? That night, for the first time in many months, he slept without dreaming.

The *Felix Roussel* was at its moorings. A colossus of a passenger ship from the Roaring Twenties, decadent almost in its beauty and opulence. The war had made a troop carrier of it, but it had lost nothing of its French *hauteur*. Its implacably first-class section, the boat deck, was strictly reserved for officers and POWs. He was about to leave Suez, the days had been more luminous. This would be his last voyage, Suez–Durban, with a swift stop

39

at Mombasa. Cities with names found only in atlases, sounds from an old geography lesson – the unknown took the colour of something familiar. As familiar as the colour of the hundreds of soldiers who came on board in full kit: black. Black South Africans heading home from a war they had nothing to do with. He would not see them again until they disembarked. In the mines they had worked side by side; on this boat the decks were hermetically separated.

Then they set out across calm seas to energetic music. Bands took turns to play, everyone sang, drank to each other. Wives and children would await them at dockside. Durban, South Africa. The war years, who even mentioned the war years? Gershwin and Frank Sinatra, Vera Lynn and Marlene Dietrich was what they longed to hear. The *Felix Roussel* granted every wish, a floating pre-war advertisement. He lived between dance floor and deckchair. In the afternoons he often slept on deck, though the ocean provided little relief from the heat. The ship rolled gently, and the hazy blue sky enhanced the illusion of a holiday. A few days out of Durban, the afternoon lethargy complete, the ship's speakers suddenly bellowed: *Un homme à la mer!* Man overboard, Man overboard! They slowed immediately, swung round, tossed lifebuoys into the sea. A lifeboat was lowered, the crew handed out binoculars. That vast expanse of water. On board the world is comprehensible, the ocean an orderly territory, something you pass through and which carries you. But one step beyond the rail and space swallows you, drags you down and down to no bottom. Anyone who falls or jumps is irrecoverably lost to the horizon. With open eyes into the maw. The search took hours, the ship moving in circle upon despairing circle. Twilight rose from the waves, and the lifeboat was hauled up. The captain announced that they would resume their course. The ship's horn blew, a salute to the dead sounding and resounding across the sea. One buoy was left behind, the twilight turned to night.

Guus. Throughout the search it was Guus he saw. A man overboard. In the chaos that followed the torpedo's impact there had been Guus' serene jump, the carefree look in his eyes. Peering through the binoculars, thinking again and again that he could see a head above the waves, he became entangled once more in the loss of his camp friend. Wondered if he had done enough calling and asking among the survivors. The raft he had plunged in beside had been his good luck, he had grabbed the hand that pulled him from the water. Saved, but Guus had not turned up anywhere. Given up on, missing, drowned, found elsewhere and carried off, died later in another camp, felled by a bomb or by disease? In Guus he had never observed uneasiness or dissatisfaction. His life had progressed in what seemed an untroubled equilibrium. Acrobat of the dependable, the normal, the visible. No high-flown words or philosophies. His hair parted down the middle. In Bandung their lives had become indelibly interwoven. There had been little room for play, the guards hard as steel, yet it seemed to him that they lived there with a greater freedom than ever, remarkably mobile. In the months before they were chased into the jungle of Thailand they had plotted their survival, spoken of their histories and their dreams, constantly in each other's company. Guus, man of a well-planned life, of family traditions, knew no despair. Made his judgements without illusions, yet was not harsh. He, on the other hand, was forever on the move, restless, with magnificent ideas about independence and adventure. Those months in Bandung had been the bedrock of his salvation. If it had not been for Guus, his wildness would have destroyed him. Guus had seen his anger, his impatience, his lack of planning. And he had taught Guus to seize opportunities, to be reckless if need be. To jump into the sea, for example, as though leaping from the pier at Scheveningen. And he had done so, confident, unafraid, self-assured – and yet gone, lost.

It was quiet at the dining-saloon tables. The course had been resumed, they skimmed hurriedly away from the seaman's grave. It had been the pantry boy, a young fellow still. Depressed for days, and then into the deep. Even the music fell silent that evening.

Two decks below, the soldiers hung over the rail and whistled and waved. Durban was looming, the shore close by. A black woman sang a welcome especially for them.

Her voice drifted over their ship, and no-one could escape her song. The melancholy was unyielding, he was lost in the native melody, the swaying, suffering song. She stood there like a mother, waiting, singing full of a longing, extravagantly, her arms held high. The men clapped, shouted, stamped. This was their town, here began the country that they had missed. Slowly he walked down the quay past the waiting wives and families, thousands of people who looked at him and at the officers and greeted them. The *Felix Roussel* emptied out behind him. Turning, he saw what he had not wanted to see: men and women in each other's arms. Homecoming. The happiness exploded all around him and brushed him aside. If only he had a motorcycle, if only he could ride into the polders, through the night again, and find her quite by chance at home. Mouth to his mouth, tongues of fire, godless, holy moment that had never passed. He was back in South Africa, back to his old, scorched dream. Alone.

3

He left Durban without delay. He made his way to the place where he had lived, Johannesburg. But he was declared unfit for work underground, and the people he had known were no longer there. The war had grazed the country, no more than that. And a railroad in Burma was nothing to them. Had he been on the move for five years only to end up here again? He travelled on to Lourenço Marques, in Portuguese East Africa. Guus had family there, he remembered, and he liked the sound: Lourenço Marques. The city lay with its belly in the ocean and was a display case of carefreeness. Portuguese and Spaniards, American tourists, Africans, Englishmen, a very different Africa from the one he knew. Less Calvinistic than Johannesburg, more cheerful. It had everything he needed, nothing that reminded him of the past, a city without memories. He found work at the Casino, a refugee's false paradise. He started at nine each night. And often, when he left at five or six in the morning, he forgot to go to sleep. The haze over the ocean, the beach without people still, in his white, bartender's dinner jacket, feet in the water, he strolled there with the surf pounding in his ears. The mirrors around the Casino bar reflected a stranger. Amidst the stacked glasses and coloured bottles he ran his little alcohol shop, tamer of nightbirds and gamblers. His crew cut from the camp had grown out, his face was handsome as before, only his eyes were different: expressionless, dull, with dark circles as though he never left the shadows. It stood out against the white of his dinner jacket. There were always women sitting close to him. Miner's overalls, camp uniform, dinner jacket, he did not consider the sequence progressive. He was thirty-three, the age Christ was when he left Galilee. And he had come no further than the Casino at Lourenço Marques. He lived, for the time being, in a hotel on the boulevard by the harbour. Every night in the game palace was like the next. A Spanish orchestra played in the ballroom beside his bar, the same repertoire each night. Across from him were the roulette tables and the half-moon tables for baccarat. The babbling click of the little balls, the "*faite-vos-jeux, rien-ne-va-plus!*" Silent winning and even more silent losses in a smoke-filled room, a bonfire of hopes. "All for the bank" was how it generally ended. Winners were few and far between, losers kept coming back for more, like life it seemed. He loved it, the roulette charged with rituals and adrenalin.

45

The semi-darkness of the saloon, the waking dream, the frivolous self-deception.

Sometimes, at dawn, first light skimming across the ocean like the gleam of a knife, he saw the head fall. No more than that, just the furious sweep and the fall. The men around him deathly quiet, the Kwai still dark in the pale morning. He stifled his memory with all the pleasure he could find. Which was not hard in Lourenço Marques. The girls from the Casino Cabaret and the men from the Spanish orchestra lived in his hotel. When they were not sleeping, they were drinking to each other's health in the lobby. On hot afternoons, a soft saxophone, strangely intimate, would drift in through the open windows. November, 1946, an eternity from Nagasaki, light years from Bandung, close your eyes and it was snowing in Holland. He had bought a pre-war Citroën for a song. At around five, he would prop a few people into it and drive to Hotel Polana, their favourite seaside café. The cane chairs and the spotless white aprons of the waiters, the military band that played Cole Porter, the strollers, the girls' voices, idleness and lounging. The nights and days of Lourenço Marques, dreamless, free, the old vision of independence now urging itself upon him again. He had never known a summer like this one. Here he would like to take his chances, here perhaps his unrest would dissolve. The work he did in the Casino, could he not do the same on his own? Without too much forethought he went to the Banco

Nacional de Portugal and borrowed the money he needed. Told the manager his life in brief outline. Anyone who had survived three and a half years in a Japanese camp, the manager decided, had stamina enough to start his own business.

He opened an American Bar not far from the Casino. American tourists, shunning poor, bombed-out Europe, flocked to the African coast. They raised their cocktails to him now as he had drunk to them in Japan and Manila. Once a toast to freedom, now a nod to the free and easy.

The ceiling fan was the only sound as she walked in. At four in the afternoon there was no-one there yet, he was reading the paper in the darkest corner of his bar. A woman entered, hesitantly; with the bright sunlight still in her eyes, she could not see him at first. He stood and asked her to come in. And whether she would care for a drink. She walked towards him, slowly, cautious almost. On impulse he shook her hand. She looked at him, startled by this unexpected warmth. He asked again what she would like and prepared the tea-and-lemon without a word. The streets were all but deserted at this hour. The tourists still sheltering from the sun, the American Bar's clientele only trickling in after six. In anticipation of that moment he would usually sit alone. The emptiest hours of the day, the most vulnerable, when he was not always able to control his thoughts. An awkward, suppressed longing for his childhood, Honk, life under a bell jar. The dreadful feeling that paralyzed him at times when he thought of his father and mother. All the years of resistance melted in one moment. His memory sprang backwards like an antelope.

The woman sat down at a table near his. The heat hung between them, there was only the whirring of the fan. He saw her looking at the photographs of Lourenço Marques on the wall. Pictures from before the war, Portuguese townspeople laughing beside a tram, a colonial house, a stadium. Local colour to keep the naked walls at bay, a reflex from the days of his father who always wanted "something on the wall".

Her eyes were the eyes of the Dutch girl, the same direct gaze, searching, challenging. The sublime moment once when he had taken her hand, the triumph when she did not turn away from his kiss. The girl he had ridden to on his motorcycle, only to lose her. Where was she now? Here, almost, a woman like the one opposite him is what she must have become. Hesitant, elegant, attentive.

He had served her tea and they resumed their silence for a while. Time and again he was overwhelmed by the old vision of the motorcycle girl. Everything reappeared, one face opening up a vista. A glance, a faltering step, a hand in his at an abandoned hour; four o'clock in a bar in East Africa, and in that same millisecond he was back home, had never left, never been in a camp, in a dark train, on a torpedoed ship, at a bomb's zenith.

"Has your café been open long?" she said. The word "café" stung him. He gestured all around, the tap still gleaming, the ceiling un-yellowed by smoke.

"Been open two months, already a graveyard of ambitions," he answered with a smile.

Most of all, he watched her eyes. Questions, new questions, their words clinked against each other. Expectantly, like glasses filled with ice. They talked for two hours, nonstop. Two hours during which no-one left their room to come to a bar. A solitary car went by, vague shadows flickered by the entrance, voices walking past, the distant shriek of gulls over the sands. Since the exhilaration of Manila, with the woman who merely listened like a well in which his story echoed and vanished – since that time he had not spoken like this with anyone.

"Africa. So why Africa?"

He had never actually told anybody, not even Guus, where he had first acquired his fascination for Africa. She had asked the question *en passant*, immersed in their conspiracy. He had never really understood it himself, his passionate admiration for the man with the Nietzsche moustache and the weathered face. A miracle doctor, an organist on tour, invited by his father to play a concert and spend the night.

He had entered through a side door, slipped into a dark wooden pew. The people around him looking inward, eyes shut or staring. The music into which he had come leaped in all directions, belonging nowhere. The whole church effortlessly conquered by one man who sat pumping at the organ. Commanding sounds, commanding man. Music for the devout, of course he did not like the organ, but he could not deny that this organist played wonderfully well. The heaviness was gone, it sounded effortless, did not appear exalted. Generally speaking, it was music for the deceased, but this concert put an end to his prejudice.

The little man in the front row, the one-eyed officer forced into civilian order, thanked the audience for its kind attention after the final note wavered and disappeared. And the organist for his performance. Brisk nod, quick handshake and his father led the musician with the moustache down the aisle. The audience stood, they walked through the ranks, inspecting the troops, his father and the organist. Out of the church, heading for the reception at Honk, their house. He arrived there much later than the others. Honk was like an altar in the night, candles at every window, little lights along the wide front steps and around the columns that framed the door. Even from a distance he could hear the buzzing of voices, a violinist, laughter. He hesitated to go in, had no stomach for the obligatory chit-chat, the refinement of it all. He walked round to the garden, to collect his courage under the cover of darkness. He listened, watched the shadows, the trotting in and out of the helpers. He found a lounge chair, sat there looking up at a starless night, his mind brewing. He was battling against the life there. People only followed in his father's wake; the man had decorations, knew everyone.

What was he to do? He could not breathe, did not want to become like the others, his father, his brothers, his friends. He braced himself against relentless coercion to toe the line. The creeping pressure to some day find a job, marry, fill the buttonhole on his lapel. There in that garden he realized how great his antipathy had become. Honk was a fairy tale, a cardboard dream. This was no longer where he belonged, however terrible the searing of his longing later, when he thought of the house. For months he had known he would skip his final exam, useless as it would be for the life he had in mind. He would travel, wander, away from good manners and tradition. Freedom, sorry better than safe, on a motorbike, on a ship, on the loose. Wild ideals, frayed thoughts about the masterpiece that would be his future. The lounge chair at the back of the garden was his domain, a look-out post for a reckless independence. He soared, and observed his flight from the oppressive little town. Footsteps on the gravel path put an end to the reverie. His mother came and stood beside him, looking back at the house, their grand, dignified, exceptional Honk. Years later, he thought of her in the house, at the piano, untouchable. Saw her coming home, hands in the pockets of her short fur coat, wordless. There was a melange of shadows in his head, without context, without order, without sound. His mother was made of shards. Later still, in the darkest years, darker even than those of the war, he felt only pain when he thought of her. A soft kind of pain, which some people call love.

"Come on, Rob, let's go in," her hand rested against his cheek. What he wanted most of all was to hold her, to listen to her voice some more. It was a silly wish, a child's craving. Her voice, the velvet choker at her neck, her gentle piano playing: it would penetrate him to the bone, accompany him till his death.

Of course they walked into the house together, into the party, towards the charged, animated little groups. That is where he saw him: a German farmer perhaps, or a Polish mineworker, if he had not known that it was Albert Schweitzer, heralded on posters throughout the town for weeks. He was from Alsace, a no-man's-land. Late fifties, sunburned, crumpled face. Wrinkled jacket, light trousers, a clearing in the forest of dark suits. His father led the man around as if introducing an exotic orchid to tulip growers.

"*Mein Sohn Rob. Sucht das Abenteuer wie Sie.*" – he was caught off guard by his father's German. Schweitzer studied him. "I'm not an adventurer, as your father believes. If only! I row down the same river, in the same boat, to one and the same village – hardly an adventure." His father was about to say something, but was distracted by someone tugging his sleeve. Now they were alone for a moment, and he dared to ask him a few questions, half in German, half in English. The man began to speak about Gabon, the forests and savannas, their unsettling beauty, but before he could get into his stride his father had borne him off again. The officer and the organ grinder, the double-breasted mayor and the healer of the poor. Father with his trophy. His brave, tiny, unreachable father. How slowly he drifted apart from him, how unavoidably did he want to hurt him, shake him off, alienate him. He was seized by an uncontrollable urge to walk away from him and vanish out of that one eye's sight. The one-eyed king of the city. While on patrol in Aceh he had been shot in the head, one eye left, and in the hospital he had jumped out of bed when the general came to visit. Saluting in his pyjamas, one hand hanging beside the flimsy shirt, one hand held up to his badly wounded head: present, always present, never absent, never afraid. During the bread riots in his town, the crowd had marched on the mayor's house. He remembered how his mother and they, the children, had been sent to sit behind the stove; it was made of iron, would protect them. Enraged folk at the door called out for his father: there was bound to be bread in their house, the bigwigs always had enough to eat! That sort of tone. And how his father, surrounded by policemen, then invited the stoutest rabble-rousers to see for themselves if there was any bread there. Their fury when they found nothing, the way they went outside and shouted: "Aim for his left eye, boys!" – that was his good one, of course. And how his father had looked at the police commissioner with that good, piercing eye and spoke the solitary word: "Charge."

He knew the story, had re-enacted it with his brothers, had told his friends about it, he could see it in his dreams and he often did: *Charge*, his father distilled to a few letters.

The officer and the pacifist, the dagger and the pen, the rapier and the bandage, he saw them walk past the aldermen, past the directors and commissioners, the pastor, the notary. Everyone was attentive, just a little more polite, just a little more cheerful. Like bees the two moved from flower to flower, but his father brought the honey himself. The reception did not go on for long. People left for home in good spirits, relieved, into the windless night. They had seen the great man, spoken to him even, shaken his hand. The violinist stayed to the very end, playing on modestly, inaudibly almost. Schweitzer, his father and he sat in a side room, beside the hearth. A fire in springtime, that was just like his father. Glasses of port, sounds of clearing up, the scraping of chairs and tables. The organ man spoke. Africa flared up. Never before had he listened to someone like him. Gabon, the very name of the country was an exhortation. Gabon was the distant corner where Schweitzer had settled. Up the river in boats, the unpredictable river, straight through the jungle. At the mercy of the current, the rocks, the narrows and the waterfalls.

The journey to an ever-receding outpost, deep in a godforsaken forest. He was promoted to miracle doctor, magician, a magnet for expectations and hopes. And they came, from every corner of the country, from forests further afield, days away from there. Mutilated, ill, half-dead, always humming. The river was his life, the village that he built was his future. His homesickness for the black continent was irrepressible. As soon as he set foot in Europe, he became out of sorts. Playing a church organ as best as he could kept him in check. Music for rituals, stemming from the desire to skirt death, to sound a keynote and lay a foundation. He gave concerts to raise more money for his hospital.

"Philosophy behind it?" his father asked, but it sounded more like an order.

The man from Alsace did not hesitate: "Lack of scepticism, a surplus of energy, the feeling that the world has lost its balance. The compelling belief that *I* have to do something about it." He grinned at his interrogator's puzzlement, and apologized for his irony. He explained how he was bound by an overpowering urge to lend meaning to whatever he did. And how impossible it was, in Germany or anywhere else in Europe, to find a god for his faith.

He looked at the two of them, his father and the strange doctor. And at that moment he opted for the organ man, the god seeker, for the receding horizon. For the journey against the current, the untrammelled, the impossible. This Schweitzer seemed of a quite different calibre from the people he knew. A quarter-turn away from a life in step. The marching had begun everywhere, in the miracle doctor's Germany the masks were lifted off and the first camps were being built, but the organ man marched to his own rhythm.

His father was not as impressed, or at least did not show it. He knew the jungle too, he knew the tropical heat and the elephant's warning trumpeting. But not for a moment would he consider stepping out of line; he believed unconditionally in administration, in discipline, structure and hierarchy. Yet there was kinship between the two. Each caught a glimpse of something in the other that he did not understand. The way they spoke of how night fell over the primeval forest – oh, later he would understand it better than anyone. He noticed their peculiar alliance. The soldier, armed to the teeth, out hunting rebels, camouflaged, blinkered by a fear kneaded into courage. And the doctor, his back to the enemy, deep in the jungle between water and sleeping sickness, leprosy and death, tirelessly performing surgery in a log cabin. From the side room they heard the violinist stop playing and pack up his instrument case. The silence he left behind was like the music he had played.

Africa and Aceh sat side by side, smoked their cigarettes and drank their port. He said nothing, just wanted to be part of it. He would tell his father he was going to Africa, or perhaps to the Indies, who knows, as long as it was away. Down elephant trails instead of up the stairs of some office. Looking back on it, that evening must have been the final push. The musical wizard with his almost tender touch had ensnared and, at the same time, freed him.

"One afternoon I was on the Ogowe River, heading north. At six o'clock there, darkness pounces like a panther from a tree. On both sides the hippos surfaced, peaceful monsters passing by without a hint of aggression. It was still light, but the darkness was already coiling. The heat was a little more tolerable, the wind had got up, birds were shrieking, and their colours glistened along the banks. And suddenly I was struck by a tremendous awe of all living things. Around me I saw only life, everything and everyone wanted to *be*. The desperate, meaningless struggle to survive, and the hippos slowly drifting by in their almost helpless motion, brought on an overwhelming feeling of reverence. Converted by hippopotami – better not tell them in Germany!" He laughed, the wizard. His father did too, raised his glass: "To the hippo, to freedom, to the future."

Lourenço Marques would soon awake from its afternoon slumber. Customers could come into the bar at any moment, and he would have to abandon the woman opposite him. Her name was Muriel, and she would come again some time, she said. Where she lived? She looked at him, tentative now, and did not answer. His story and what he had not told her were the bait he had tossed out, without his realizing it. What she did not see was the hook beneath his words. Now she was the one who offered him her hand, and she walked away, without hesitation this time. For a moment she paused at the entrance, as though to get her bearings. She did not look back, but quietly disappeared from view.

4

He found no trace of him. The few Dutch people living in the city had never heard of him, nor was his family known to anyone. Sometimes, when he went sailing off the coast, alone or with Muriel, he felt the urge to keep going, to follow the waves. Water on all sides sharpened his sorrow for what he had lost. Someone was looking for him, someone called his name, a head bobbing, an arm waving, a raft thudded against his boat. He had been dreaming, imagining things in the heat of the day.

"The sun is your worst enemy," Guus had often told him. And indeed, the most unequal fight of his life had been against the roaring sun in Java and Thailand, a sun that made your ears hiss and crackle. Your mind grated, the heat spun around inside your head with no way out. Guus could tolerate it better. *Lekas, lekas,* hurry, hurry into line, countless hours of waiting, standing. The dull thump when someone fainted nearby. It was forbidden to turn your head, to look about you. Guus forgot once. Half turning, he joked in a whisper that whatever they did, they must not faint, for the Jap would send them to another camp. Bandung, 1942. They did not even see the blow coming. The squat sergeant felled Guus before he had faced forwards. He lay curled up on the ground, lifeless. A sharp blow to the neck is effective. You are more or less dead, but after only a few moments you are able to stand again. The anxiety he felt that Guus had been killed, his frustration at not being allowed to help him. He saw how his friend opened his eyes, slightly puzzled, and how he slowly resumed his place in the ranks. Unnaturally friendly, almost irritatingly civil, he rose again – a miracle of equanimity. A hand through his hair, dusting down his shirt, the ruffle in the roll call had passed. Hardly ever had he seen a man react like that. They became inseparable; his life with Guus had begun. Guus who had never known uncontrollable passion. An aristocrat, self-assured, raised with the same mores as he. But without his contrariness, without his rage. Guus had, he said, gone to university at a time when Holland's eastern neighbours were stoking the flames. But you ignored them. Shut your ears. Jews, Sudeten Germans, Austrians, vague rumblings all. Concentration camps, refugees, the Japanese in China: all matters of record. Vienna, Munich out of kilter, what was there to do? The Nuremberg Laws, book burnings, Kristallnacht; newspaper stories. Yet he was not insensitive, far from it. It smouldered, and he smelled the danger. And just in the nick of time he had taken a job in England. The London office of Shell, in one of the city's suburbs, was a table spread for young academics. With war in the offing they crossed the channel in hope of work and adventure. Guus described the atmosphere, the deadly normalcy of office work, and the blazing days in the summer of 1940. Sandbags in front of the Houses of Parliament and government ministries, barrage balloons above the city, army units on the streets. The war seeped into every crevice, it made every conversation more intense. Yet he would remember that summer as an oasis of freedom. The over-flowing pub, where he stood debating each night after work, was the barometer of those days. It was calm still, after the battles on the Continent and the flight from Dunkirk. The sun shone on a waiting and watching London, hard-blue skies in July, strained light in August. He did legal work for a firm that looked beyond the bounds of Europe. No war without oil, no campaign without petrol, that was the neutral observation of a large multinational company. The cinemas were always full, jazz clubs and theatres too, the newspapers kept running extra editions. You are an actor learning your role, you are a journalist writing your story, you are a publican drawing your beer. Outside it is stirring, outside it is lurking, outside the invisible train is rolling. Guus fitted effortlessly into a city preparing for the worst. The air-raid shelters built with such haste warned, but did not alarm him. He was twenty-seven, free, no wife or children. His flat in Camden was paid for by Shell, and he had managed to buy a grand piano second-hand. He played in the evenings, the window open onto the little oval park where people read their newspapers during the day, or just sat. He played as though his life depended on it. The music came from within – there were moments when some of the chords made him want to cry. During those months he practised every piece he had ever learned. His built-in reserve was unwound by Rachmaninov and Chopin and Mendelssohn. They were months of detachment and surrender. Churchill's speeches were on the radio everywhere, and he lapped them up. News of the impending German invasion, reports of the tenacity of the British Army, punctuated by cricket results. Guus lived as never before. His measured Dutch life was a distant memory. Music, war, oil, pub, and the inevitable attack on London, Guus felt caught up in a galloping, glorious moment in History. He loved to see everything in the light of History. How would people some day speak of the era he was living through? He had the ability to think himself out of his own time. He dreamed of stepping into a time machine, travelling into the future, forward, not back. At odds with that was his piano playing. Music is memory, irresistible nostalgia. At his piano he was back at home; as he played he saw how he once had been before the world opened up, before the books and the music, before friendship and chaos: the essential state, the secret of his equilibrium.

The first time the city was bombed he was in a meeting, working overtime with a group of men at the office. It was a Saturday afternoon, 7 September, tea on the table, there was talk of going on to dinner, seeing a film. The air-raid siren howled through the streets, but there was no reaction. Cars kept on driving, buses picked up passengers, no-one ran. The sirens were for others, some streets away, it had to be a mistake. The delusion would not last. Shockwaves rolled through the boroughs all the way to the suburbs. The docks were burning, it rained bombs, the heart of the city steamed and boiled. Later, in the pub, he was told there had been at least a thousand aircraft, a cloudburst of hostility. When the next attack came that very same evening, there was not a soul on the street as the siren sounded.

He perked up amidst the growing danger. Particularly at night, in the small hours, the bombs would come sailing down. The caprice of an aircraft opening its bomb bay. A signal from the gunner, the push of a button, the pilot at the same time dodging the searchlights. It was a land of shadows up there, high above his house. A deafening empire of power dives, rattling machine guns, tongues of flame. Guus would sometimes sit on his balcony in the dark, watching, the city blacked out around him. He despised the alien pilots, seeking out lights on the ground.

They dropped their bombs randomly, sometimes way before, sometimes well past their target: London. Sealed-off streets, blackout paper everywhere, people in shelters and the Underground. Creeping away, if they cannot see me they will not hit me. But in those August and September weeks he heard about tens of thousands of dead and wounded. Unknown, unseen, but still dead beneath the rubble, reduced to ashes and grit. Sleepless nights in Camden. Exhausted, he went to the office in the morning, hoping it would still be there. He took a different route each day, trying not to become downcast by all the shattered houses. But in the end it was always the same route, so he would not have to see the extent of the damage.

First the siren coming in over the breeze. Then the sinister silence, the waiting for the drone of the planes. The swelling roar of sounds. He sat on his balcony, the September heat still nestling against the house. Occasionally a siren would wail, only to stop abruptly at an unseen nod, or a simple defect. A bomb came down a hundred, maybe two hundred metres away, on a row of houses. He had just decided that it was getting too noisy, and that he should go inside. Halfway out of his chair he was slammed back into it, echoes rattling in his ears. Flames leaped up at once. He ran there, but could do nothing as the heat was immense. Fire brigade, police, ambulances, a stir as though it were broad daylight. By sheer luck no-one was killed. The people who lived there were out of town. He stared at the burning house, at the story of its occupants flickering away. Picture albums, children's drawings carefully preserved, heirlooms, their first china. He stood there motionless, staring, and could not prise himself away from the fire. There was no panic, everywhere you felt the stubborn resolve not to be intimidated. You were absorbed by that resolve. The defiance grew in your bones by contagion. Your weakness evaporated, your natural urge to flee. You wanted to join the airmen up there, or the air defence. But you knew that for a Dutchman it would not be easy. Perhaps the fire brigade would take him, and after that he would seek out the Dutch army, enlist. That night, on a London street, his piano stool went up in flames, his freedom took on the hue of a uniform. He was perfectly calm, perfectly sure of his decision. Back home he wrote a letter to his boss at Shell. A leap forward. And a leap into the abyss, into the dark-green waters of the Formosa Strait.

The water splashed onto his back, the sun shone fiercely, the Indian Ocean lay enticingly open at his bow. Sail on? His friendship with Guus had become the compass needle in all his doings. Missing, worse than dead. Vanished without trace in a few metres of sea. It had been a circus trick, the way Guus stepped off the rail, in a reckless attempt to look upon the world as a playground. His own leap had been more effective, as far out from the ship's hull as he could manage. He could still conjure up the fall, seconds long, down towards a black, undulating mirror that shattered on impact. A few desperate strokes, clutching around, grabbing the raft, it had all happened in less than a minute. A straightforward disembarkation by the look of it – by the book. Jump, look for raft and move away from the ship as quickly as you can. The *Bungu Maru* went down sullenly, indignant. Ships are humans, are feminine. From his shaky plank deck he screamed Guus' name, cursing him sometimes, wildly and in every direction, always his name. Until the three others aboard the raft had had enough and calmed him. Waves ferried them away.

The dinghy he had bought on a whim he christened *Diroha*. Sounded Swahili, people said. But it was only the first two initials of his and his brothers' names, painted once on the childhood canoe they had used to paddle around the town's port. With Muriel he sailed whenever he could. Always out to sea, heading nowhere, and back again. After her afternoon visit to his bar ("You called it a café, Muriel, a *café*!"), she had reappeared a week later. Same hour, same empty bar, same order, new sensation. He had called it "the Earl Grey incident". He put the tea on her table, she stood up, looked at him. Everything he had told her the week before lying between them as an embrace. His arms around her, a kiss on her lips, they seemed caught in an etching, their hands clasping, their eyes dark with intimacy. So strange, so close, so inexpressibly sad their embrace. He felt himself drifting towards an abandoned past, but she stopped him and said: "My tea's getting cold." Muriel, phantom of the motorcycle girl, the starry sky over Drenthe where she had stood in the early morning and pushed him away. Into the adventure, into the morning mist, the journey home at the average speed his father had been so proud of. His father, the mayor, buried in his absence, dead and not risen again. Not risen again to talk to him about the Royal Dutch East Indies Army, the secrets of survival in a jungle. His resolute father, his waved away, discarded father. He had scarcely spoken to him after the evening with the organ man. He had sat listening in open admiration then. The fire in the eyes of the two old soldiers, bayonets in Aceh, hypodermic needles in Gabon. The mystery of shaking off his father. The mystery of his unrelenting stubbornness. He searched for the cause of the change in him, for the origins of his dissidence – and every time came back to the girl who looked away.

Sailing with Muriel, Lourenço Marques and the white Casino on the beach behind him, before him the endless ocean. Sail on, sail on, never to moor again. Spare sail, water supply, biscuits and fruit, enough for weeks on end. In former days he would not have hesitated, he gave in to every urge. An airgun in the classroom and he let it off. Motorcycle from the shed and away he raced. Train going at full speed and he would clamber onto the roof. Punched, he hit back. Always alert, grabbing every chance, never shy, always the first on the scene, never retreating, never neutral. The years in which he opted for a way into the wilderness, although he did not know quite how literal that would be.

Muriel tightened the jib, he had the mainsail, rudder loosely in one hand, head held high. The slow waves slid by, the bottle-green swell of an inhospitable sea.

Guus' family did not live in Lourenço Marques at all. He had simply imagined Guus mentioning the town, or perhaps they had listed all the cities they hoped some time to see? L.M., as the American tourists called Lourenço Marques for short, L.M. was wonderful. He had his doubts. Was it really that beautiful? If there was no trace of Guus, or even his family, what would keep him here? Muriel, yes, but she was as footloose as he. Mid-thirties, divorced, no children. Her life adapted to whatever presented itself, not docile, but with the nod of an expert. No hint of anger or rebellion. She had chosen a life with little homesickness, prepared to travel on as and when.

Wind and water and the two of them in between. Space enfolded them, no room for time, the hour silted up. They went for a sail whenever they could. Sailing; he knew all the rules, learned when he was a child on the Dutch lakes – second nature, just like skating. His movements sure, he led the sheets across the boat, unfurled the sails, pulled in the fenders and shoved off. Before long they had become a team, sailing for their lives. Loose and calm in the afternoon, when the sun beat down. Making headway in the early morning, before the heat arrived. And silently uneasy when evening came and lightning flashed its sudden warnings. That summer of 1946 was an unforgettable one – not that he would ever forget a thing. Being unable to forget is an illness, and he had carried the symptoms for so long. In the goldmines he had scarcely been able to keep his longing for home at bay whenever Yoshua talked about his mother. He had seen the mother at the boy's funeral, he had taken her hand and pressed it to his cheek. She did not speak, simply let him. Yoshua, who had been his friend for a few months, and whose eyes had followed him through the jungle. The echo of his last words in his ears, the strange sound of death in them. That mother. The contrast with his own mother could not have been greater. A woman raised at the edge of the Kalahari, and a woman brought up in a house with a music room. But each with a son who was no longer there, would never be there again. His mother who had waited from the day he left for news, letters, a telegram. The moment he had almost boarded the *Oranje*, back to Holland, to his mother. The irreducible emotions when he had stayed behind and the ship disappeared. Impotence, anger, relief, always those three.

During the years in Thailand and Japan his memory was gradually excavated. Guus was the only portal to his past. Standing beside each other at roll call had seemed like happiness, Bandung an academy of friendship. The never-ending days of the camp, with the European riff-raff gorging themselves on memories.

While he was digging for gold in South Africa, Guus was casually strolling the streets of his college town. Everything he had avoided and at times despised, Guus had done. Guus had acted out the grand showpiece of the gentleman student as if this was how it ought to be: *tableaux vivants* by a club president. Cane, hat, three-piece suit – uniform of a future career. Not a trace of shyness, not one wrong step, an immaculate vocabulary, waistcoat, watch chain. Evenings and nights were spent at the club, where his word, as president, was law. The roar struck him whenever he opened the leaden door and climbed the steps to the dimly lit hall. He was hailed from all sides. His major-domo had saved a chair for him beside the fireplace that was always in use, Dutch gin and beer were brought without being asked for. He called out to two young students who were twisting and tugging at each other's ties, and began his nightly vigil. Exhausting months, great training for later.

But he much preferred coming to the hall at eleven in the morning. Sunlight slanting into the room, the reading table still in shadow, the newspapers spread about. The barbaric night was still in evidence here and there in the little heaps of shattered glass, the room smelling of beer. The silence was unreal; you could hear your own footsteps,

70

the bar shone with new bottles and glasses. The subdued calm, the objects hanging and standing there had been hanging and standing there for a hundred years. The copper candelabra with their pale light, the trophies, banners, paintings, relics of dreamed and forgotten glory. They hung and stood in shaky balance, but had an indefinable grandeur. No-one to hail him on those mornings, no-one to disturb him in this mausoleum of optimism and success. Around him the tables were being set for lunch, the engine gradually gathering steam, the first club members already appearing. Guus listened patiently, heard the places being set, the cutlery carefully arranged, everything as if covered in thin gauze, spell-like, there was nothing to distract him. This was how it felt to play the piano, to disappear into music, into a sea of sound. President of a club, the trappings of a genteel life, Guus found a shallow pleasure in them. Well-trodden paths or music, he would choose both if he could. At anchor on a watch chain or in the lap of a composer – both please. The months to come in a blacked-out city were still far, but not that far off. The attentive reader of the newspapers on his reading table could detect the echo of an abyss, a dismal composition, timpani, rolling drums, thunderclaps. Guus read, Guus listened. But the nightlife of a president was subject to law and order. To a self-imposed discipline that shaped his days like a concrete mixer. Lord of the country's largest pub, with the wildest nights in a fortress of self-assurance. Studying with roaring fires all around, shadowy portents on the paperless walls of a delirious club, future good old boys.

Those mornings at the big table were beacons in Guus' memory, beacons of luxury and uneasiness. Luxury, for they were days of unbridled freedom and hollow pleasures. Uneasiness for what was brewing, what was changing. But there was not much talk of it. How the Jews had to flee, how in Germany only one voice was heard, only one arm raised. The flush of terror in that land, the years of unfathomable silence.

The newspaper table told no lies. Guus may not have talked about it with his friends, but it built up inside him. He suppressed it, but beneath his waistcoat and behind his watch chain, he felt the threat shifting restlessly. He readied himself, studied, tried not to think about leaving. The cosiness of his student life, the cushion of the friendships around him, the good-natured ways, the perfect harmony with his father.

Playing the piano was the only thing that took him beyond that shelter. He practised, sometimes for hours on end, when his housemates were off at lectures and it was quiet. The ancient grand inherited from his mother took up almost his entire room, his breakfast plates usually stacked on its top, a small desk wedged in to one side. The remaining space he crammed with paintings, antiques, curios. The knotted burgundy carpet was hemmed in by heaps of books. He looked out upon a canal, the Academy building, the graduates café. The carillon that had rung out across that canal for centuries, over the shuffling caps and gowns. A view down on hollow, passionless thinkers, scholars who saw nothing but would frown away the future into learned manuscripts. Sometimes he hated that blinkered world of learning. No-one there shouted for help, no-one sounded the alarm; down in the furthest reaches of their libraries they remained silent, benighted, dumb. And meanwhile, everywhere else, it had begun; Italian trains running on time, the *Sturmabteilung* marching through Germany.

He played the piano, to hear as little and to feel as much as possible. Plans for his departure took shape slowly but surely, he would leave before the bubble burst. All those nights amidst the bellowing of his contemporaries, all the mornings in the peaceful hall, all the hours at the piano: it added up to a profit and, inexplicably, there was a parallel loss. He wanted to leave.

He was handed his degree on the day of the Munich Agreement – the corruption of the word peace. A nameless sorrow blew up, a storm of betrayal. Munich, watch him leave the city, arrive in London, see how he descends the steps of the aeroplane, triumph in his buttonhole, a breast pocket filled with vanity. He impaled Europe on the walking stick of his blindness: Chamberlain, prime minister of all Britons and right-minded persons, dressed like Guus' father on church holidays. The early autumn came, with finely knit sunlight. At four in the afternoon the canal lay quiet and abandoned. 29 September, 1938, his last hours as a student. His father was there, of course. They had stormed the café; he was one of the first in his year to graduate. The farewell rituals of the privileged, the laws of imagined solidarity; raised upon shoulders, high above the ground, fearlessly he put his name on the wall of the Academy building. Never alone again, never again without title, welcomed wherever he went.

"Guus!" – his father was sitting close to the covered billiard table. The exhilaration of the graduation toasts had dwindled. That evening they would all come together again, the hall at the club would be blue with smoke, a president's leave-taking meant breakage, new furniture and swinging on the chandeliers. Someone would climb the stairs on horseback perhaps, they might order a round of rumpus, and piles of plates might be raining down from the gallery. And he, Guus, would climb onto the big table and be wheeled through the hall like a steamroller. Garlands around his neck, collar unbuttoned, jacket torn: the popping of champagne corks echoing in Munich. Boot and saddle, sound the attack, peace is an old woman! "Chamberlain, in vain, in vain" they would chant. The unbridled courage of the pint glass, the drunken stagger of despair.

"Guus!" his father beckoned and pulled up a chair. The café was at the edge of the light, the canal still lit by low sun. And they, inside, sat in silence for a while. They began sentences that crumbled before they were completed. Guus and his father, simply sitting there, letting the twilight come closer. As they had done so often at home, in their large house on the IJssel. But even if their conversation faltered, if their words were blunt or void of elegance, they did not need much to feel at home in each other's company.

"The rook came back." News breaking from his father's front. Behind it lay everything Guus adored. The grounds, the woods near their house, De Kolkhof, the enormous weeping beech next to the coach house. The countless times his father had come home with a roe deer across his handlebars, ducks or pigeons in bags behind the saddle. And he had helped him pluck the shot birds in the kitchen where the water still came from a hand pump. The soft down of short feathers you would pull from the bird, still resisting, the furrowed pigeon skin beneath your fingertips, the fragile neck. His father was an excellent shot, and already as a child he had accompanied him to the elevated hide. In the evenings they would wait for hours without moving. And it was not the moment of the shot, but the mysterious wood with sounds of invisible animals that he most liked to remember. Then he finally appeared, the old buck, at the end of his life, in line with the glistening barrel: the shot never missed, not once.

"I didn't know he was gone." He had tamed the bird himself, years before. It would sit on his shoulder whenever he fished in the pool. To him the idyll was normal, he did not know better. Living on one's own land, with a gun licence, dogs on the pantry step. There was no other place where the piano sounded as lovely as in his room at home. The high walls softened the sound, rounded its edges.

Guus told his father he would not stay in Holland for much longer.

"I want to go to England, I'm applying for a job with Shell."

"You'll have to leave the piano here, I'm afraid." There could have been no readier approval. His father understood, endorsed the idea, lived too close to Germany not to comprehend the danger. The hubbub in the bar rose again, regulars were dropping in now that the students had left. The board was lifted from the billiard table, cues taken from cases, cannons commented on. Occasionally they had to lean to one side to make room for a shot. And so they were drawn into the workaday world, forged together at a table steadied with coasters. Both happiest of all in the water meadows of their river, both sure that it would be a long time before they would walk there again, shotguns open in the crook of one arm, dogs out in front, the smell of freshly cut grass all around.

Hay wagons on the road in front of the house, men with

scythes, the rattle of harvesters. Summer on the IJssel, sometimes drifting to town in a wherry. It had been his last summer at home, buckling down to a long essay and finishing off his studies. It was too noisy in his student flat, the evenings there went on too long, he could not put a word on paper. Weeks with his father, as never before. His mother had been dead long since, he could barely bring her to mind. It did not trouble him, he was used to coming home and finding only his father there. That summer he worked at his father's desk, in the room of his youth, a room he would describe in Bandung as "the room of rooms". A domain where every object led an indestructible life, watched over by his father. There was the built-in cupboard with his guns in racks, a short one for magpies, a doublebarrel for pheasants and ducks, a heavier, single-barrelled rifle for roe and stag. And the walking stick with its telescopic rod concealed ingeniously within: a poacher's rod. He had picked it up so often as a child, unscrewing the tarnished copper head and letting the rod slide out. And of course back in again quickly, before the warden could see you.

Dark-green wallpaper, dark-green velour curtains, the little antlers of roebucks nailed to planks, with the year written beneath. A Voerman riverbank scene on the wall, a bookcase built around the door. Decoys, boxes of shells, a dog basket, a Frisian wall clock, chairs and tables with the sheen of the nineteenth century. The gun room, the study where he worked those last few weeks. His father had turned it over to him, saying "It's more peaceful" – a gesture of deepest affection. Guus had studied there as in the palm of a hand. Admitted to the most intimate universe he knew. Sometimes he laid his head on his arms and slept at the desk, ten minutes, no more. The inexpressible calm around him when he awoke and looked up, immensely pleased to be there, to hear his father working the dogs or talking to someone out on the road.

The canal, too, was dark now. The billiard players tiptoed around their table, bowing over it like subjects before an emperor. Their eyes prowled after opportunities to score, a dry tock to the neck of the ivory and the ball shot back with spin. Guus stood and fetched more drinks from the bar. He raised his glass to his father's: tomorrow things will be different. Silence, a glance, two mouths swallowing. The moments in which so much contracts, how to see them, endure them, how does it all vanish, where does it leave you. The end of the future, a speechless past, no more dreams. How to make sense of this, these seconds of extreme lightness, all of it irretrievable, unrepeatable. Guus and his father, they were watching. For a moment, a storm, the wind blew soundlessly across their river, the weeping beech trembled, a door slammed shut. Inextensible day, inextensible night, a flight of stairs to eternity. Otherwise nothing, otherwise no-one. Eyes speaking, two glasses raised, everything in between. As in the palm of a hand.

"Where will you live?"

"London."

"When?"

"A couple of months, maximum."

"Rent a piano."

Between oil and music, Shell and Chopin.

"I'll see you off – where do you leave from?"

"Hook of Holland."

No more now, please. Just the evening, the shouting for no reason.

"Are you coming tonight?"

"No, the train leaves at nine, I want to catch it. The dogs are alone."

5

Muriel asked what he was thinking. Nothing. Everything, really. Guus' disappearance. The leap, the hinge – in retrospect – of his life and his survival. The Bandung months, the age-long days in which they had been hounded by the Jap, kicked and drilled. But they had been grand. Snapshots of the grain and joinery of their alliance flashed through his mind, sailing on the ocean, summoned up by the waves. The stories Guus had told kept flowing. Muriel listened with one eye on the sails, ready to tack, sail through the wind, to cast anchor if need be.

But he could not carry on, did not want to. Lourenço Marques was an empty town, his American Bar only busy in the summer. The season was over, the tourists had left for home, for America. Every afternoon he sat waiting for customers who never came, all through the winter, evenings were pointless. The doctor he went to see found nothing. The vague, hollow feeling that reminded him of the hunger in Thailand – he was unable to explain it to the physician. He had suffered and borne everything – mines, heat, beatings – just to feel ill here, dull, displaced! Talking to Muriel helped, but not enough. In her arms he dreamed for a while of being gone, back on Java, back in Holland. It never lasted long. The night tempered his malaise, but never enough. How to tell Muriel he would be leaving Lourenço Marques, and her? He had spent weeks searching for the right moment. He did not find it, and months went by in long silences.

"So when are you leaving?" she asked finally.

He had just fastened the mainsail, and looked back at the distant harbour.

He had left the motorcycle idling, his hand on the girl's shoulder, farms in faint outline across the fields. Details of the clothes she wore, the colour of her front door, a dog approaching and barking. The brief exchange, his incomprehension and her resolute rejection. The cold on her cheek, which he caressed for a moment, her eyes with their dark brows. Portrait of a lost life, his life.

"Without me you have a future. With me only a past, illness, unrest," he said without looking at Muriel. The spring wind tested the sails, and water jumped high against the boards; they had to brace themselves.

"I'm planning to sell the bar and go and see whether there's still something for me in Johannesburg." The journey back, the sails reefed, the sheets pulled in. "You shouldn't come, maybe I'll come and see you every now and then. We'll keep an eye on each other, won't we? Muriel?"

She nodded, raised her eyes, saw nothing. There were no words for this farewell that she had been anticipating for so long. There was no way to fight the hollowness in his body, no remedy for his memories. She had no antidote, no solution, her courage was not great enough. She would manage alone.

Johannesburg, Jo'burg. Terrible city wracked by unemployment, districts full of poverty, paintless tower blocks, wretched wasteland, all worn out. Black ghost towns under the dictatorship of mining directors. Since he had left eight years earlier, Johannesburg had become the Hell of the North. He did not know which way to turn. His old neighbourhood had burst its seams and lost its centre. Townships burgeoned around the goldmine where he had worked. All the shine was gone. If gold glistened anywhere in this country, it did not glisten here.

The girl at head office looked at him with pity. Employed by the mine eight years ago? It was as if he were talking about the Ice Age. There were ten applicant for every job, he did not stand a chance. It was as though the war had merely shifted fronts, ending up in the outskirts of Jo'burg. He walked out without a word. He passed the gate where Yoshua had stood each morning. Presumably his mother still lived somewhere in that sea of zinc-roofed houses; did the boy's father ever come round? Always on the move, hireling of the horizon. At the short funeral ceremony he had spoken a few words about Yoshua, about the months they had gone down the mine together. The mother was a religious woman, absolute surrender to the will of the Almighty. Not a sparrow fell to the ground without His consent, no human being – Yoshua included – died without a divine purpose. After that, he would never be short of purposeless dying. Rounds of rumpus, Chamberlain, in vain, in vain. Upsy-daisy and your millions tumble into their graves, heavy with purpose.

Yoshua's mother had sung at the graveside. Swazi hymns, impassioned, strong, on the edge of breaking. The love, the tormented music, the mother convincing herself. Just as the woman at the quayside had sung the *Felix Roussel* into Durban, ship of his return and definitive uprooting. They had streamed ashore like a lava flow of emotion and embraces. He had been shaken by the overwhelming reunion, soldiers' wives and children weeping with disbelief and joy. He had stumbled into South Africa with a duffel bag and a suitcase and the haziest of plans.

Yoshua and his mother, his glinting boots in the dark shaft so many years ago. Yoshua, his helper, his little lamp-bearer. The way they had gone into the lift together day in day out, trundled down 1500 metres. Yoshua who opened the door for him, stepped out ahead, cheerful and alert.

On his grave he had laid flowers, along with the box of matches Yoshua had been clutching.

"Never lose the matches, boy!"

"Never, Boss." Quick as a snake, yet caught by a stupid blast, lit perhaps by the breath of the Eternal. His mother sang, but not with clenched fists; she wept, but not to accuse anyone.

Office Girl could not have known as she watched him walk away, could not have known who was walking there and how long for. It had been a mistake anyway, trying to get back his old job. Even the smell of the mining office was almost unbearable. Up until the bookkeepers on the floor above it stank of mine, of despondency, of stale darkness. Repugnance mingled with melancholy, grim desolation reared its head. Jo'burg had become an impregnable fortress. He got by on jobs that lasted no more than a month, two at most. Now and then he dropped a line to Muriel, until her replies dried up. Contact with Holland was rare. His mother wrote letters which he answered sporadically, his brothers only returned his silence.

His attempts to track down Guus met with a dead end. The "proper authorities" had him registered as "Missing, 1944, Formosa Strait". Stubbornly, he read "missing" as "lost", "temporarily misplaced", "not yet returned". There were cases of men who appeared years later. Stranded somewhere in the heart of Thailand or Burma or Japan, settled in a village, met a woman, and apparently untraceable until further notice. Soldiers who left the jungle long after the end of the war, not knowing whether it was over! But Guus? Washed ashore, recaptured, hospitalized, liberated? He would have sent word, surely he would have sent word. A native woman seemed too far-fetched for Guus. They had shared their stories about women, but never that indiscreetly. He had never spoken of the motorcycle girl, had brushed aside questions about his mother. There in Bandung, dreaming constantly of leaving, going home, or at least away from Java. Dancing in the "Shanghai Dream" for as long as it lasted, fleeing to the city with girls from everywhere. That was before he met Guus, before the Indies fell. Bizarre old Bandung, in the Preanger Highlands that were still considered unassailable, packed with refugees, adrift in a pool of rumour. The Japs had landed all over Java and were driving the Royal Dutch East Indies Army ahead of them. There was not much fighting. He did not even know if Guus had ever fired a shot. Rob certainly had not. All they could do was wait, or cruise the valley in small patrols. As a sergeant in a motorized battalion he had a bike with a sidecar. The heat skimmed across his cheeks, a haze hung over the paddy field in early morning. On a motorcycle the tension was less tangible, and he experienced a kind of freedom. Hollow freedom – the catastrophe at arm's length.

Guus' unit had arrived in the city on one of its final

days, he said. Sent out from Batavia to end up in the fantasy world of Bandung. Where there was dancing at parties in the Casino, where the restaurants were bursting at the seams. Bursting. If only he were still in London, if only it were still September 1940 in the beleaguered city, bound, besieged by bombs. Nowhere the same sense of doom as in Bandung, where the bands played as though on the *Titanic*. Each night, for weeks on end, the Heinkels had blown in and laid their ribbons of fire across the city and the harbours. "We shall fight on the beaches, we shall fight on the landing grounds, we shall fight in the fields and in the streets, we shall fight in the hills; we shall never surrender." Churchill snarled at them, drove them on, kept them on their feet when they felt like lying down, a word for a word, a tooth for a tooth. No-one surrendered, no-one slept when he should have been awake. Guus had wanted to be part of it, to join the R.A.F. "Never was so much owed by so many to so few" – he wanted to be among those few, in a Spitfire, up and at 'em. But he did not make it through the selection; no-one was keen on an untrained Dutchman. He volunteered for the fire brigade, an army by any other name. Generals of the night, colonels of the pump, soldiers with lorries, hoses and fire boots. Never have so few extinguished so much, pulled people from beneath rubble, given comfort, provided rescue. His sleeping he did by day, at night they chased through darkened London on their way to the latest strike.

There he stood, but no longer atop a large table, fire hose in hand to spray groggy students out of the club. In the dead of night, wearing a helmet and heavy gloves, facing walls of fire. They whipped each other to new levels, every night they worked faster, rolling out the hoses, attaching them to the pumps. Choose positions, eliminate risks, locate time bombs. Side by side with men from the ambulance service, reckless, in hellish tempo, without a word.

Sometimes, off duty, he would walk over to Curzon Street, to Heywood Hill, an intrepid bookseller. It was a little monastery of volumes on antique tables, with a few silent people behind desks. A world presumed dead, a cave the sea could not reach, a *fata Morgana*. Up the steps, through the door and he was stepping into De Kolkhof, as it were. There was even a dog on the doorstep to trip over if you wanted to. Fragile as parchment, an empire of bookmarks, it whispered all around. Great Jesus of Nazareth, people were actually reading and studying there! A stone's throw away all sorts of things were going down; houses, people, animals, whatever. We shall carry on regardless, no need to make a fuss. A bookseller sells books. Heywood Hill's bookshop seemed an enclave for habitués, Guus saw always the same people. Orders were placed, books fetched, people searched through shelves and in tall piles that were crying out for balance. A secret society that met in the shop's twilight. Heywood Hill, the last remnant of imagination still intact. He threaded his way amongst the books, conscious of every step, every movement. Picked up a novel, flicked through it, smelled the paper. This was how paper smelled, this was how it used to be. His father's bookshelves smelled like this, the university library, the improper fragrance of spare time. All far behind him now; everyone he knew and loved seemed to have been made infinitely small and stacked away. His life had room only for air-raid sirens, speed, fire brought under control. Except for there, sleepwalking amongst the books under the war's lee. Enlightened moments on Curzon Street.

No, Bandung was decay, a playtime of shrivelled expectations. They wanted nothing but surrender, nothing more than to come to a halt. The *Titanic*, the last meal, days of all or nothing. Guus could not bear the apathy, and still hoped for resistance. Don't let go now, don't capitulate, for God's sake regroup, pull yourselves together, close ranks or, better still, attack. But his simple passion ran up against fatigue and cynicism and fear.

He was there when the Governor General of the Indies climbed out of his car, back from signing the surrender to the Japs a day's journey away. A man out of a book, a character from the theatre. Blue-blooded to the last, bold as brass and undaunted. In England you would see any number of them, products of a certain upbringing; he recognized it in his father. Mohicans on their way to the auction of their little empires, the downfall of their oases

of fine manners. Guus had looked on as the G.-G. walked
into his mansion, cool as marble, and saw the servants
bowing like puppets in a shadow play. It was three in
the morning, 9 March, 1942 – the Dutch East Indies had
ceased to be. Guus was part of the small unit that guarded
Mei Ling, the large official residence outside Bandung
in which the G.-G. lived after he left Buitenzorg. With
its round turrets, Mei Ling could have passed for a hotel,
just as everything around there reminded him of holidays.
Even at night the heat hung in the trees. Guus had
difficulty getting used to it. The hours on guard duty,
staring out at nothing, listening for nothing, he found it
demoralizing. In town there was singing, officers in dinner
jackets drank whisky at their clubs, their women jingled
crystal jewellery – so much sham, so much dust in one's
eyes, so much deception. Guus thought about London;
it had been snowing there for two months already, the
radio reported. Whatever else happened, the weather
reports continued. The weather in Europe, snow in
London, everyday things filled him with longing. The
flight of geese above the IJssel, in perfect formation without directives, swerving, vanishing into the evening sky.
Or a canal lit up by a red sun, casting shadows into the
cafés. He had heard nothing from his father. Occupied
Holland was sealed tight as a drum. There had been a great
deal of bombing around where he had lived, De Kolkhof
would be a fine target. Guus entertained few illusions. The

Boche would surely have flung his father out of the house. He would have buried his weapons, loaned out his fishing rods. "What about you?" he had asked his father at their farewell. "Renew my shooting licence," his father had replied laughing, "so at least I'll be allowed to shoot back." Too old to leave, too young to do nothing, he would see, he would see soon enough. His house, his tenants, he would keep it going for as long as possible. "But maybe Chamberlain will be proven right, Guus, maybe we'll be lucky."

At night around Mei Ling he was a heartbeat from the fall of the Indies, yet he thought about snow in London, in Curzon Street, snow covering his fire station near Hyde Park, covering all those stretches of the city bombed bare. Streets he had raced through in a red fire engine that were blocked already the next day. The grid of the city changed every night, every hour, an invisible cartographer shifted the routes and led them through the wilderness. If only he were still there, said the hissing in his head, he would not be here. The inescapable, sticky heat, the whining crickets, the grinding and shrilling of the indifferent countryside around him made him solemn and anxious for the first time. From England to the Dutch Indies, a volunteer in the Royal Dutch East Indies Army, quashing the enemy; this time his beeline planning had got him nowhere. Except into the arms of the Jap, the protective arms of Nippon, malaria and typhoid fever, camps and jungle. It was over, Bandung had fallen without a fight. "And when you're lying in the trenches, afraid, just remember that God is beside you in the mud," the field chaplain had said just before the fall. Trenches? Mud? The good man must have forgotten that World War One was over, that fighting was the last thing to be happening. The mud would come much later, in a different country, under the devastating sun of Thailand, land without God.

"Name, rank, unit – date of birth, address, nationality" – curt questions from the Jap, and a little later they were lined up for roll call, battle array of the vanquished. Foot soldiers in the most literal sense. Stand, wait, saunter, shuffle, stand, wait, saunter, shuffle, crippled cadence of a day in camp. Bandung, oh Bandung. The war was raging there still, foot by foot it crawled upwards, nestling in the loins first, then in the back, pouncing on shoulders and neck. Roll call in the thrumming sun, funnel of heat, murderer.

6

Johannesburg bore no resemblance to the place where the great adventure had begun. Soldier of fortune, ha! Soldier of luck, soldier of destiny, soldier of fate: take your pick. Soldier perhaps, but fortune and luck had dragged their feet and fallen too far behind. Soldier of fate, ill-fated soldier, ill-equipped in any case. Lying atop that train, no more than sixteen, he had already felt the need to head in another direction. A strange urge to open the carriage window and climb out. Exhilarating freedom on the roof of a carriage blasting through the countryside. His hair blown back wildly, his eyes teary, his body light. The landscape in little blocks, fences as far as the eye could see, villages and steeples on a bolted-down horizon. He could not stay there, could he? Below him the shouts of his travelling companions, laughter, waving from their window.

The others.

A doctor he went to see found nothing, just as in Lourenço Marques. But he knew there was something, the void kept growing, a deep listlessness he had never known before. No, nothing wrong, just his imagination. Could it be the war, was that it? Missing family and friends? Rubbish, what would a doctor know about such things? A doctor's business was the stomach and intestines, bones and evil humours. Friends and family, Guus, Muriel, his mother, Yoshua, the woman in Manila, the organ man, the motorcycle girl. His father. The clippings office of his memory was hard pressed to keep up. An endless series of little reports tapped out by a hysterical radio operator. His life was stuck together with memories – never intended, never thought he would, not like that, never. Good luck and fortune, that would be his fate! He was thirty-eight, a new life in a resurrected world should be on the stocks. Damn it, he was not getting anywhere. No train to carry him, triumphant and ecstatic, through the fields and on to the next station.

Cape Town, he would go to Cape Town. Where he had arrived so impetuously by ship. The two suitcases he had shown to customs were no longer his. All he had was a stumbling block and a smokescreen. Once again he found himself standing before colossal Cape Town Station, a single step and homesickness would seize him. But he did not take that step, Holland was no longer an option; he would see his mother there, and then what. Then nothing.

He could not go. Not mend time, paddle back upstream, re-enter the railway carriage, roll up the window, put the crow back in the tree, ignore the organ man.

The organ man, what could have become of him, he wondered as he walked the long road to Cape Town harbour. If there was any work it would be there. He passed the war memorial, not far from the quays where the prospective dead had embarked for Europe. A man cast in iron, rifle at the ready, ready to shoot, ready to die. Anonymous man with your anonymous thoughts and your anonymous youth. He did not pause, but saw the monument and how untrue it was. The dream of a sculptor who had stayed at home. Never had there been such triumph, never such readiness, never arms like that, open to the enemy's charge. I attack, who follows? – more like, I follow, don't attack me! Mr Sculptor had never known the war, never seen a jungle, never taken shelter under bombardment, had survived no camp, no torpedo in the ship, no waves.

What had the organ man been up to during the war, he wondered. He had known all about the jungle too, had lived in the backwater of Gabon. Would he still love his God and his villagers? Flung far from time and space, smacked down on the banks of a muddy river in Africa, did he still breathe and play his harmonium amidst the lianas? What had it been about the man that had so attracted him that night in Honk? Walking the quay and smelling the ocean, he was back, sitting in that room with his father and the stranger. A breath of fresh air, a gust through the provincial town where his father ruled the roost, where no wind was ever felt. His being here now was doubtless hatched in those days. Fire in the hearth in spring, the violinist in the background clicking shut his case, a noise like a shard in the silence. No god was mentioned, and Africa lay wide open between them. Schweitzer; loner, rickety soldier, solitary maniac. It had become dark in Honk, they could barely see each other, the standing lamps shed little light, but his father's eye had glinted. The words spoken that evening now seemed no longer important. What he had retained were elusive wisps. Isolated chords, the organ man's handshake, a few shavings from a story of dark Atlantis. And his vast admiration for the man, out of all scale, without knowing why. Perhaps simply because he was a match for his father? A clash of little kingdoms, a contest without stakes, their unspoken appreciation. That evening he opted once and for all for a different life, wilder, more compelling, more complete. The stranger won out over his father, and even his mother. He could still see their silhouettes, still hear the sounds from the kitchen; he disappeared, had never seen the man again, his memory stopped.

The ships he passed looked soulless, his longing for the sea was gone. The unpainted iron, moored by thick ropes, was almost irksome. He wandered aimlessly, supposedly in search of work. Something was stirring in his bones, something was not right – but he would not go back to the doctor. Beside the water was one place he still wanted to be; he returned to the harbour again and again, not to take ship, not to arrive, but because it was a no-man's-land: no belonging, just being adrift. Edge of the town, edge of the continent, the sea like a misty hand he did not grasp. Harbours and ships had been part of his life for as long as he could recall. The little canoe with the exotic name, unsteady balance between two paddles, immeasurably far from the *Felix Roussel* or the *Alcantara* or the *Bungu Maru* or the *Tegelberg* or the *Cape Town*. All of them once on dockside, once anchored, once waved farewell. So many seas, so many gulls in the wake, so often disembarked. At least his father had been spared the war, but then he had been through one of his own. His old papa, deep in the Acehnese interior. With a handful of bearers, ten bayonets fixed and one mission.

In a drawer of his father's desk he had once found a small notebook, wafer-thin, its cover shellacked. The mystery of that desk, the motionless objects within and upon it, gallant bits of flotsam from an age gone by. Etched in his memory was the afternoon he had walked about in his father's study and sat at his desk. There was no-one at home, his brothers off skating, his father was running things, his mother had gone out. Everyone was somewhere, doing something well defined, everything moved and worked, life was a flywheel, driven in one immutable direction. Church bells rang, he heard the shouts of children throwing snowballs, saw the snow on the house across from Honk. A leaden grey afternoon, the rooms unlit, the wood of the furniture reflecting no light. He sat there in nothingness, feeling lost in his father's empire on which the sun never set. He was only a boy at the time, fifteen, perhaps sixteen years old. It was not long before the storm came up that would never subside. Now there was still that enchantment, the drawing power of his father, the officer, the cyclops, the bruiser. Idly, he opened and closed each of the desk drawers one by one. Silence ganged up around him in the dirty marble light, uneasiness came over him as he crept, without leave, so close to his father. The desk at which he always saw him writing speeches, papers, letters. The hieroglyphs of his father's life; the blotting paper, the inkpot, the sharpened pencils in their special box, the oil-black telephone. In the bottommost drawer, beneath yellowed documents, was where he had found the notebook. He opened it and recognized the handwriting immediately, no-one in the world had a more lovely hand. A booklet of no more than eight pages, some blank, a few written upon. Would he read it?

The harbour at Cape Town, what was he looking for? Backwards in time, away from the water that spoke to him of the ocean, of Guus, of the dying years. Rather back into that afternoon, smeary hour of snow in the street and almost thaw and indecisiveness. The sudden, accidental discovery, the surprise at what he read. In pencil was written: "Thursday – 5 o'clock – attack from all sides. Not much chance of holding out. Regards to my Mother and brother" – and then his father's name, only his surname. See, that's just like him! Writing calmly in the face of mortal danger, in a scuffed little notebook, of his imminent death. Shots, screams, ambushes on every side in unknown territory. "Not holding out" meant skinned alive, impaled on a stake, throttled. "Regards to my Mother" – mother with a capital "M". Regards from Aceh, regards from the darkened forest, regards from a lost post, back to back, rifles loaded, cartridge belts filled. How had they been saved, how had they "held out"?

He read the preceding page: "Following scimitar attack of Tuesday (2 dead, 8 wounded), halted here due to shortage of bearers." So they had been there for two days already, before the attack on Thursday. Bearers dead, so of course they could not move on with all those wounded men. Scimitar attack. Written with a firm hand straight across the page, matter-of-factly. Notebook on lap, rifle against knee. Logbook of the final minutes. And then, on the third page: "4th Brigade, home at 15.30 hrs." – and that was that. Home at 15.30, half the men dead or wounded, fear beaten back, an escape route found, rescued at last? Not a word on any of that, nothing extraneous, no sensitive matter, no wasting of time. Up against it, death not far away, little chance of holding out, regards to Mother. But then: 4th Brigade, home at 15.30 hrs. Tempestuous were his feelings, tempestuous his thoughts. He put the little black notebook away quickly, as though he had stumbled upon something forbidden. Like an archaeologist he restored the desk drawer, put everything back precisely where it had been, and carefully closed it. Never saw the notebook again, never referred to it, but he had come across his father's spirit in an unlikely recess of his paperwork.

He stayed in the port area till it was almost dark. At one or two shipping firms he asked if there was any work. Gradually he resigned himself to taking what he could get, as long as it did not have anything to do with a ship's hold. From Muriel he had heard nothing, not for months. His departure from Lourenço Marques felt like the start of a freefall. Something was driving him downhill, his memories took on the gravity of basalt. Muriel had been a ledge on his descent. She had walked into his American Bar out of the blue. It was she, Muriel, who had travelled through the night to meet him, not the other way round. It was she who had raced through the icy-cold polders, eyes full of tears and hands half-frozen, to him. But only in a manner of speaking, of course: change "icy-cold" to "humidly hot" and for "polders" read "African veldt" and alter the time and place and mood. Let it all disappear, disembark and dissolve. Peel off the skin, erase the scars.

How he must have longed for a woman to come and fetch him, how he must have imagined his life changing hands. And when she was standing there in his bar, he wanted her so badly to be that woman. Muriel had not even noticed him, he had taken her hand before her eyes had adjusted to the dim light. And she had not turned around and left him on his motorcycle in a cold that would never go away. Muriel was the polar opposite of the motorcycle girl, who had uprooted him more than he would ever want to admit. Her rejection had crippled him. He had simply stood, his hands clutching, frozen, at the handlebars. He had not turned on his heel and ridden off at all, not in the way his painted memory had distorted it. He had called out her name as she walked back into her house. She had shaken her head, "Bye, Rob," and shut the door. End of Act One, the curtains dancing against each other as they fell, the silence before the applause, the bated breath. He could not remember how long he had waited, hoping that she would come out again. Ten minutes, half an hour, the polder wind cutting through him. It had been the primer for his flight. The race back to his parents had been the last; after that it was full speed away from them too.

Muriel might not answer his letters, but he still enjoyed writing them and did not really expect anything in return. As though tossing messages in bottles upon the waters. The fatigue over which he had no control only grew. He frittered away his days at the harbour. There were no jobs anywhere, nothing was working, and he refused to clean ships' holds. For a former mineworker, a ship's hold was no depth at all. But he would find Guus there, the *Bungu Maru*'s alarm would sound as soon as he descended with the cleaning crew. He had become an open wound, a battleground of memories.

It had been pure luck that they made it out of that hold. First up a ladder surrounded by hundreds of men, in a panic for the open air. Guus and he, one right behind the other amidst a ring of elbows. In grim silence they had wormed their way through the ominous howling, below them, above them. Guus in the lead, his white hair like a beacon in the darkness. "Straight to the rail, don't wait, don't look down too long, just jump!" he had yelled to Guus. They had been forced to stop again and again, crushed together, squeezed into a space smaller than their bodies, it seemed. The narrow, unlit corridors spiralled up and up in an endless trek of push and pull. Cabin doors stood open, through the portholes he saw the drab, rolling waves; the sun was not up. The ship's contractions had begun. They were squeezed upwards, headlong, water gushing into the hold beneath them. The listing of the ship threw them hard against the deckhead, they could scarcely keep their footing. The lifeboats had been lowered, the Japs already rowing off, not the greatest of swimmers. That was something for those arrogant Westerners. If they wanted so badly to stay alive, well then, grab a plank, build

101

a raft, take off your shirt and sail. Time would tell who or what was left over for their Emperor. The relentless pace of it all. A momentum in which time exploded. As though the world did not touch him, so mechanical did it seem, everything meshed with minute fineness, not a moment's hesitation anywhere. Whoever hesitated was doomed, whoever paused to think was lost. Every action, every step was taken involuntarily. They were there, they stood there swaying. For one moment though, the iron stroke of the torpedo attack froze in midair. Just before they jumped Guus saw a dog sliding in their direction. He had grabbed hold of it, said something to it, tried to calm it. As if he had found it lying on the pantry doorstep, that was how Guus had bent over the animal and stroked its ears. And let it go. They watched as it spun away from them, hit a turret and vanished. A dog that belonged to a Jap, a boatswain who had taken him to sea years earlier. "Go, Guus, go!" Then the moment came. Then nothing else.

Days he spent walking or sitting at dockside, his head filled to overflowing, his body as drained as back then along the Kwai. On the move for almost fifteen years, to arrive nowhere. "Hireling of the horizon" is what he had once named Yoshua's father. But the hireling's pay was now a problem. He was living off his war pension, wrested from the authorities and deposited in the bank. The humiliation to get that money he would rather forget. He had had to prove that he had been on the Kwai, torpedoed, liberated in Japan. He had been forced to fish papers from the bureaucracy's intestines. Even the Japs had been called upon to search their camp documents. In the middle of that damned forest, every man had been counted, profiled, immortalized. Their bookkeeping had been as flawless as that of their allies. Yellow-skinned Boche, kowtowing Huns, the pencils in Bangkok as keen as they were in Berlin. Bookkeeping, a silent branch of warfare. Clerks at the heart of the battlefield, no-one escapes *their* tallies. To be written down, to be indelible, to have escaped from it all but not from the long reach of their desks. His name had been there, clear and cold in angry chicken scratches, the conclusive proof of his presence, then, once, a continent from here. His name stripped down to a pair of sticks, bridges, blots: penned in Thailand by a soldier, a boy almost, a little machine that thought it was doing its duty. He remembered the afternoon he had been profiled and questioned: he had been ordered to give the name of his mother, the name of his father, when and where he was born, his army unit, where he had surrendered, his profession before the war … it was all still there. He had handed the papers over to the "Honorary Consul of the Netherlands" in South Africa. It was the unscrupulous denial of his time at war, not a word of it touched bottom, the written detail meant nothing, was a story, soulless. But it did the trick. For five years later he received his soldier's pay to the day: taken prisoner then and then, liberated there and there, annual pay so and so much, missing property such and such, seven thousand guilders in all, seven thousand one hundred and sixty-five guilders, to be precise. Joyless calculation, joyless remuneration, he could live from it for a while, but for how long, and for what, really?

Back to his bare quarters on Clifton Street, where emptiness and gradual neglect were piling up. Out of the door each morning, back again by nightfall, the last sunlight high along the mountain's crest – a steady loss of ground. His father's military manual contained the most beautiful sentence ever written by a soldier: "Repeated halts are not conducive to the steady gain of ground." Quoted freely within family circles: brothers who lagged behind on a cycling tour; mother pausing before a display window – "repeated halts ..." It was all still there in that rudderless mind of his, he took everything with him, no matter how often he struck camp. To 22 Clifton Street, or to 10 Corridor Coorde at Bandung, wherever and whenever: packed to the rafters with irreplaceable sentiment, useless memory, thoughts pulled out of joint.

In Jo'burg, where he had lived between day and night, his days spent underground, in Jo'burg his rooms had been as unadorned as they were here in Cape Town. Even then he had avoided furnishing his room, fearful of the unrelenting association with his parents. As a mineworker he had soon earned enough to buy things, paintings, lamps, a desk. But he did not. Most things in shops he considered ugly, and beautiful objects he simply ignored. The Dutch house, Honk, had to disappear at all costs, had to remain locked away. Nothing was to look like home, like stately order, any more. The entrance cordoned off, sheets over the furniture, cords slung across the chairs as in a museum, depot of a forbidden past. Emerging from the mine, walking through the twilit city, through the door of his local on Rissik Street. Blown away, wriggled away from the little officer and from his mother, his impossibly sweet mother who never stopped writing letters, bottles of them on the waves of the Cape of Good Hope.

"Hey, Dutchman, you coming along to the dog races? It earns better than those damned mines of yours," – and he went. With thousands of others on rickety stands in a hurricane of voices. For months he went, until one day he lost a bundle and stopped right then and there. He liked taking chances, his whole life was a gamble, but just then he could not spare the money.

On Clifton Street he thought back on his Jo'burg years, in his cell-like rooms looking out on a crowded street, mountains in the distance, the ocean out of view. Slowly but surely he was being pushed off the continent. For five whole years he had been able to hitch himself to the goldmine, to Jo'burg, to life in a boomtown. Until the war broke out and he signed up, with a sigh of relief. Yes, it's true, he had gone into the war with a sense of being

105

lifted to a new order. Voluntary service, cheerfully off to an immense theatre. But he had no desire to be a spectator ever again. In Jo'burg he had not yet severed ties to the old country; he had still been the foreigner, the Dutchman. The war was to rid him once and for all of his home-sickness, of his background and his birthplace. The scorched earth, the total upheaval in the end was unex-pected. He had not counted on the Kwai, on Japan, on the annihilation.

Long evenings in Clifton Street. Cape Town, 1950, just before the emergence of apartheid. By then he knew all too well what apartheid meant, standing apart, on the wrong side of the world. Jobless, ill, torn from his past and fight-ing it always and everywhere. Marches through the streets of Cape Town, demonstrations, police beatings, all became blurry spots in his unblinking eye. For hours he would sit at the window, staring into the unscrupulous sun. His daily life began to slip away even before noon, no sense of time. He lived as though by chance, cut off from the rhythm that had kept him afloat for so long. In the mines and camps there had been the harness of an invisible clock. Descending with the first shift, the thundering doors of the lift, the hated screaming of the Jap, the iron-clad discipline of roll call. It had, strangely enough, provided a certain routine, the unforgiving rituals had poured him into a mould. And his American Bar and Muriel had given his days a cadence too. Now he was finished. There was lead in his bones, or something worse than lead. No medic could measure up to that.

The day came when he signed up to sell encyclopedias. He saw a notice pasted to a wall: *Salesman wanted.* He had finally hit rock bottom. Selling encyclopedias was the ultimate mark of failure. "Clark Gable of the Rhine", who had called him that? A girl at school with whom he had danced all evening, and to whom he had become engaged, just for a laugh. He could get away with anything, everyone looked up to him, an immoderate freedom rolled out the red carpet wherever he went. And now this: a shabby building with a storeroom full of boxed encyclo-pedias. Selling on commission. No sales, no income. They offered him a month's probation. Did he have a tie, and a coat and hat? Selling was a respectable business, the publisher demanded that the salesmen dress neatly and well. It was worse than the goldmines. Door to door, my God, ringing bells. The first glance from the man or woman who opened the door was decisive. Clark Gable, do me the eyes, how did that smile go again? After a week he had sold only one set to a Dutchman who had probably taken pity on a former countryman. The world in a box, the whole of human knowledge gathered by some squirrels and packaged for sale. He dragged around a box contain-ing twenty-five volumes in a rattletrap car the publisher had lent him. Thus he travelled back and forth across Cape Town, and realized this would be his last job. Thus far, and no further. The sellout of his smile, the decline of his charm: Ma'am, here you have the universe within arm's reach, before long a babbling brook of knowledge will flow through your household. Six days through the city, six days through a torn, contorted city where black and white never met, not unless white stopped black to check his pass. He had seen them aboard the *Felix Roussel* two decks below him, their hands on the rail, gesturing in conversation or staring out across the water. Sometimes they sang in voices as dark as their skin. Black and herded together for reasons that were unclear by those who ran the shipping line. *Ordnung muss sein*, black with black, white with white, the difference being that whites were accommodated in first class, with a three-course dinner and a dance floor. Simple superiority, a Noah's Ark by race and colour, partitions between them, that was how they had sailed. Why did no-one make a fuss? There was no-one shouting that they had all gone mad, that they should open their eyes. In their deckchairs on the best and topmost deck they had dreamed, watched the gulls gliding behind the ship, the long lines of foam it drew. The war was over, the terror forgotten – or so they thought.

Driving through Cape Town was like crossing a chessboard. Black and white squares, a city of pawns. After a week he went back to see those who had said they would think about it. Their addresses he had folded tight into his inside pocket. One by one they declined. They had discussed it, it certainly was an attractive offer and the books looked wonderful, but … By the end of the week he had all but exhausted his harvest of names, his references had vanished, torn to confetti, thrown overboard. One name remained: Batson, Edward Batson. A woman had said that her husband might … He rang the bell. The door opened. Guus! The resemblance sprang out at him. For a few seconds his friend was standing there, in the shadow of the open door. But it was not him, of course it was not him. Risen from the waves in the midst of a tidy Cape Town suburb, what was he thinking of? Nearly white hair parted down the middle, a man in a tweed coat, patches at the elbows, a cricket fan probably, well educated, the kind of man in need of a new encyclopedia. Tired and confused, he explained what he had come to sell. That damned Guus, catching him everywhere unawares, hounding him down to his last chance to turn a buck.

"Please, do come in."

Batson led him to his study and showed him one of the bookcases.

"The same encyclopedia, 1935 edition. I need a new one, the world has been turned upside down since then. If I order this 1950 edition from you, what will you give me for these?"

He had not been expecting that, had not been briefed about trade-ins. Guus could easily have dealt with this man, he no longer. Guus would have pulled one of the volumes off the shelf and asked about that lovely painting on the wall, "A François Krige, isn't it?" He however did not want to look at the room in which he found himself. There was something he recognized, he could smell it, it nailed him to the floor. The desk, the curtains, the carpet, the objects everywhere, the pain it caused was just too great. He waited, desperately wanting to leave. No sale then, no encyclopedia. A trade-in, he was not sure, he would have to ask. Guus would have fixed it in an instant. Certainly, that could be arranged. One cricketer to another, how's that?

But the transaction was completed in the end. He would bring the new encyclopedia if he were authorized to accept the old one, his boss would have to decide, it would all work out, Mr Batson. With a name like that, the man had to be a cricketer. Newlands Cricket Club, with a view of Table Mountain, he had seen them lounging in the shade of the long line of oaks, white men and women, and across the pitch the blacks, close to the railway station. The languid play of teams in impeccable whites, the insufferably slow applause for a ball that rolled across the ground at the speed of the clapping. The New Year's match between Cape Town and Transvaal on 2 January, 1950, the eve of a new war, white against black, victory to the whites. How's that?

"Are you Dutch?" Batson enquired of him tentatively. He would always remain a Dutchman, it seemed.

"I was," he said brusquely. Guus would have said "yes", and pointing to his friend, "and so is he".

"My mother was Dutch."

In an instant, he understood his distress. This was a Dutch room, full of Dutch heirlooms. Even the plants were Dutch, in a manner of speaking.

His mother too, his mother still, not so very old at that, not too old to see again. His mother was Dutch too, Mr Batson, and she lived in rented rooms and had to move all the time and her husband had already died before the war and she had a son who had lost his way. How's that, Mr Batson? I know your kind. Stick to your cricket and enjoy it while you can. After you, old boy. Pitch it up, old thing. Knock it for six, draw the crease wherever you like. Skip and run as long as you can, sprint, catch, nick the ball, take your wickets and score. Applause, slow and steady, wins the game. The blacks at the boundary say nothing, walk back to their trains and disappear into the low sunlight – do you see them go?

He stood motionless, silent for so long that Batson asked if there was something wrong. He had been clear enough, he hoped? And when could he expect an answer?

4th Brigade, home at 15.30 hrs – gone, out of this ambush, he had to get out of this room where a Dutch mother had lived and into which his own mother had exploded like a left hook.

"I'll be back next week, Mr Batson, with all twenty-five

volumes, you can count on me."

He was hardly able to find the car. The unexpected rage and regret had unsettled his sense of direction. The tweed coat with elbow patches, his father had worn the same, and his brothers. And damn it that was not his world, and damned if he could shake himself free of it, and, damn it, his mother whom he loved so much, who had rested her hands on his shoulders back then in the garden: if only he could see her again. He found the car close to a small park, not far from the house. He opened the creaky door, sat behind the wheel, did not start the engine. Deep in his body it had erupted, the inescapable. He was dying, he was thirty-eight and he was dying.

He started the car. He drove into the twilight, the evening still warm. Clifton Street, Clifton Street.

He climbed the stairs to his room. He was into the last days of his probation. Compared to the others he had sold next to nothing, and he knew that his contract would not be extended. The telegram he found stuck in the door hardly needed reading. "Return urgently desired, Mother …" He was free to go, he had to go, an alibi! His mother was dying and he was not with her. He stood in the middle of his room with the telegram in his hand. As though a geyser had been turned on in his head years after the pilot light had gone out. A stinging heat behind his eyes, no tears flowing. Void rushing full, a hissing sound. A vacuum being punctured, tubes suddenly rushing with gas. The lift, falling hundreds of metres into the depths that first time in the mine, the inexpressible feeling that your soul is still above ground while your body has stepped from the cage below. The blazing hot train carriage halting at Ban Pong, the maddening noise that freezes, the doors sliding open onto bewildering space. He stood there with the telegram in his hand, would have liked to keep standing there for hours, days if need be. On guard for his mother, a salute, an all-night vigil like the one in the forest along the Kwai till the sun came up, and the sword swept down through his campmate's neck. Waiting he had become good at, postponing, deviating, disappearing. But there was no escaping. His mother was dying and he could not catch up with her, just a little too late with his own death, he realized.

He read the rest of the telegram: "Ticket at Wingfield Airport." His brothers in action, the powers that be taking steps, ordaining a ticket he could not pay for himself. Still those invisible strings, a distant hand that beckoned. He went to the airport, he could fly that same evening. The departure hall was dimly lit, there was hardly anyone, a few black cleaners, a workaday world. The last time he had left Africa was via Durban. Bound for a liberating war, a new home, a different woman, free sorrow.

It was called simply Hotel Durban. He had spent two nights there with Kate who was "coloured", almost black.

113

Memories are always black and white: only yesterday, it seemed, she was lying in his arms. Unacceptably attractive, she was. He had not known her long, had met her in Jo'burg. Her skin was the shade of a strange desert. She wanted him badly, melted his reserves. He let her go. She even spoke of marriage, a word he would not dare to spell. When he shook his head she was not disheartened or sad. Her dark eyes, her black nakedness, were as hospitable as before. The days in Durban, the glistening hours with Kate, nomads the pair of them, strayed from the course of things for a time. The *Tegelberg* awaited, the quays stacked with cargo, the cranes swinging back and forth. But they, they were still hiding in the hotel, hand in hand, mouth on mouth, body to body. Freedom, war, sea. Nothing could get him down, he lived in a state of utter detachment. Kate was a drug, a mind-expanding substance, an elixir. He would remember her without regret or pain, she was a miracle of matter-of-factness. She withdrew from his life as easily as she had entered it. Back to Jo'burg, back to the sequel, whichever one.

Wingfield Airport's semi-darkness made his departure bearable. He sat behind a glass partition and listened to the voice from the loudspeaker. Deliverance would come from there: passengers for Europe … He had not flown since those stolen nights in Manila, when a couple of American pilots had taken him along to Hawaii and San Francisco, out one night, back the next morning. His head still full of the peace, the void of war. The sensation of flying without enemies in the sky, the droning motors cruising for a bar in a corner of the airfield. Five years ago that was, on the other side of the world, the right side. The Jap beaten, the Bomb fallen, no-one had ever heard of the radiation that racked your body for years. Manila and farewell to the woman he did not remember by name, but by the way she had listened, her breathless attention. Manila and the glorious welcome for former POWs. Ex-POW, former prisoner of war, well, well. You remained what you had been for so long: a prisoner of the war. The uniforms shed, the guns handed in, alright. The starved bodies equipped with new padding, the muscles flexed anew, hair grown back, O.K. But the Emperor on his island stuck to his guns, and the little soldier in the jungle trudged tirelessly on. He missed Guus relentlessly, how often in his dreams had he jumped to meet the waves. Bang, awake, a dream, no water, no need to shout, Guus was no longer there.

His plane was the last to take off. The lights were out already, except in the glass waiting room and along the departure hall. People were milling around him, he heard the murmur of fellow passengers. Stepping out into the evening wind, the collar of his jacket fluttered against the back of his neck. For the hundred metres to the plane across the dark tarmac, he was awake and alert. But climbing the steps to the aircraft was an absurd ordeal.

His heart pounded, the stewardess must have heard it, how could she not? She looked at him with concern too. He passed her, out of breath, exhausted. Before falling asleep in his narrow seat he thought of his mother, there in Europe. His mother in combat, or in resignation, death only a handshake away. When had he received a letter from her, when had he last replied, how many bottles at the bottom of the ocean?

7

Schiphol, Amsterdam, words simple enough for the sign-painter, simple enough for a printer or a bookkeeper or an air-traffic controller. But not for one who opens his eyes after a dreamless flight from South Africa and views the contours of a world changed dramatically.

Then he saw him approach, his younger brother. Fifteen years he had not spoken to him, fifteen years he had been out of sight. Why was he alone, where were the others? His brother held both hands in the air, welcome and warning in one. Walking towards him, he suddenly understood: he was too late.

"Rob!"

"Little Brother!"

Facing each other, hands on each other's shoulders, he heard him say: "She sent her regards, she died yesterday." He looked at his little brother, who was struggling not to cry. What had happened to him? He had a bandage over one ear, his skin was eroded, furrowed.

Regards to my Mother – mother with a capital "M".

"Was she in pain?"

"No, but she asked about you a few times, whether we knew when you were coming."

The void inside him, that leaden hollowness. Too late, the story of his life. Left his country, travelled the world, lived in every corner of the earth, and now too late to deliver his mother the final salute. The salute of his life, words never spoken, the simple ones. Her hands on his shoulders in the garden, her hand against his cheek, and the organ-man in the house, the start of the adventure. The soft pressure of her hands, the voice urging him demurely to come into the house and say hello to the guests. His irrevocable decision in that garden chair at Honk, and his mother's voice on top of that.

Again the dullness, the emptiness tugging at him. He looked at his younger brother, patted him on the shoulder: "Did anyone keep my old motorcycle?" He had to raise his voice over the sound of his brother's saying "whether we knew when you were coming". The boy looked so battered, as if he had been caught in the crossfire: white face, swollen ear, a bloodshot eye. Two years younger, he was. Back in the golden days of Honk they had played tennis, gone skating, taken cycling trips to visit family in France – in the days before the Revolution, before the guillotine, before the bloodbaths. "Nothing survives, and not even that."

Night-time at Schiphol. So very different from Africa, everything so well defined, sharp, wireless. They walked to the exit, saying little, his brother had a special pass to pick him up. At the stamps in his passport the customs man raised his eyebrows. World traveller, businessman, doctor, diplomat? No, black sheep, soldier, refugee, stranger. Summoned by his mother and arriving too late to set straight the velvet choker at her throat. The suppressed images of his mother, at the piano, her hand turning the sheet music as though gently brushing away the notes. *Liebestraum*, dream of an old love from whom he had fled. His mother, Kate, the woman in Manila, Muriel. The customs man waved them through. Phantom doors slid open and he was in Holland.

"Do you remember when Father arrived here by taxi? The *Uiver* had just landed and there were thousands of people standing at the fences. Father walked straight up to a guard, and all he said was 'Plesman', the name of the airline director at the time – as though that were the magic word that would divide the Red Sea and allow him to walk through with his sons to congratulate the crew. That was Father, to a T."

"'Well driven, Engineer' – another of his old sayings," his younger brother said.

"'Roy, we're leaving' – that time someone at the table said something untoward, and he and Mother got up and left. Why did he call her Roy, anyway?"

119

Roy, his mother. Who was dead. He did not want to think about it. He had the feeling he was stumbling, or was it just that his brother was walking so fast? There were a few things left for him to do in this country. Bury his mother, of course. He would not be able to speak at her grave, not like at Yoshua's, or the few sentences he had mumbled along the Kwai for a head on a thread. Everything he had to say was in quarantine – every word was contagious, every sentence might unleash an epidemic of nostalgia, of insupportable sorrow. He had to give his brothers the idea that things were looking up for him. They had to leave him alone, that above all, with their well-meaning families, their children, their positions. He would have to talk, answer their questions, look at their photographs, listen to their war.

"Train to Deventer, then the bus, it stops close to De Kolkhof. There's a café across the road with a playground in front of it. I'll be there at eleven-thirty, we can have a sandwich if we feel like it." Instructions from Guus' father. He had found him with no great difficulty. The train to Deventer crossed the countryside he had once ridden through on a steely cold night, and had watched waking up in the early morning. Fields and villages and patches of sandy forest lit by rays of sunlight. Guus' father was alive, thank God. A few telephone calls and he had picked up his trail. On the phone the father had let him finish speaking, nervous and out of breath as he tried to tell his story. That he had known Guus, had trudged with him through Thailand, and how they had become entwined, like lianas in a jungle, wrapped up in each other's life stories. The conversation had been brittle, full of meaningless detail on his part, he was in no state to say anything of importance. But the father seemed to understand, listened patiently, and very much wanted to meet him as soon as possible. He had asked whether that was not a problem, with the dogs and all – and then it had been quiet for a moment; the dogs were no longer there.

The IJssel, the IJssel Bridge, Guus' river. Mutely he looked out of the window, at the Church of St Lebuinus rising above the first row of houses. Disheartening, how everything seemed to exist and go on. The flames of British bombs had been put out, the piles of rubble removed, the victims buried or scarred for life, the shops newly furnished, the windows polished clean. This was the station where Guus had alighted dozens of times to visit his father, to study, to play the piano. He was about to enter Guus' old domain, his arrival, down the steps from the art nouveau platform to the exit, the canal full of swans as it should be, the bus station, the journey to De Kolkhof.

Passengers getting on and off, the sound of the engine pulling away, the stuttering acceleration of the bus, it all sounded comforting. Over the driver's shoulder he could see the cobbled driveway that must lead to the house.

The funeral, the cremation rather, was behind him, Driehuis-Westerveld, a field of urns. His father, it turned out, "stood" there too. Cremation or burial, a real doctrinal conflict he had kept his nose out of. His brothers had decided. He had only mumbled that anything was better than "missing". To which they had not reacted, of course. How could they know that he was still looking for Guus, who was always at his heels and in his path? That he was as close to him as a brother. And what is more, that somehow he had begun to see Guus as the person he could have been. Should have been, if his father had had his way. Amateur psychology, all senseless enough as it was. He had to stop trying to hitch his life to Guus'. The dark life and the light – his had become the dark one, Guus' the light. The one who had stayed behind as they floated off on their raft, the unlucky jumper, the actor, the one who must have washed ashore on some unmapped beach – you could hardly call that "light", but he did. His brother, his comrade, his travelling companion, his camp mate; alright then, his alter ego. Guus, who he was not, who he did not want to be, the boy with whom he had jumped off the ship. And he who jumped after him, never left him again, who remained hanging in mid-air. Guus, someone with a father. The father coveted in secret. A father like he once had had himself, and admired and loved. The father he had shunned, baited, insulted, hurt. The eyeless one, the little officer come home from ambushes and pensioned off before he turned thirty. Guus and his father, their happy years on the river, with fen pole and rod through the fields around their house. The dogs on the pantry doorstep. The cursed happiness of such a youth.

Mute, still, petrified, he waited. The bus took him to the last stop but one, where the father would be. Came to a halt.

Entering the café, he recognized him almost instantly. Guus, had he lived to be seventy-five. Old man, corduroy trousers, tweed jacket, hat on the table in front of him, cane leaning against a chair. The man got up slowly, looked at him, waved him over. Hesitantly he crossed the room, there was no-one else in the place. The sun did not penetrate, a few lights were burning, the curtain at the door fell back with a gentle slap. The couple of metres he crossed from door to table were a hardship. It was not pain, it was unwillingness, aversion, he wanted to stop, lie down, turn back.

"So you're Rob? I hope you don't mind me calling you by your first name. Was it Guus who told you about the dogs?"

"They always lay at the pantry door, and they stayed there too, even if a fox went by five paces away."

"You must have known my son well. Please, sit down."

Known, that was an understatement. Their stories shadowed each other, the endless hours spent on their *tatami* mats at Camp Bandung, talking elbow to elbow, moving through their lives centimetre by centimetre. Known – my God, he knew everything, more than the father did. What, after all, does a father know about his son? It is always the other way around; the son knows about his father, waits, watches, receives. The son is the beggar, the father tosses the odd crumb from his table.

Easy now, though, Guus' father had yet to get started, he had barely spoken. Give him a chance, tell him what you know, be kind, don't start protesting straight away.

"I just wondered whether you'd actually met him, and how well you knew him. I've been disappointed a few times, by people who claimed to have seen him and spoken with him, in London or the Indies – and then had nothing but generalities to offer. I know he's reported missing. The military commander on Java sent me an official letter to confirm that. We regret to inform you … torpedoed during transport from Singapore to Japan and never found … Ships searched for survivors … not found … our sad duty …

"When I brought him to the quay at Hook of Holland, summer of 1939, I warned him: take swimming lessons in London. He had never wanted to learn at home, just wanted to sit at a piano, or go hunting or rowing. He didn't like swimming, couldn't do it."

Slowly it dawned on him. Guus, it was so outrageously stupid, could not swim! But why hadn't he said so, why hadn't he cursed and screamed that he couldn't swim? He had stopped to help that dog, had spoken to it soothingly, won some time. Why hadn't he grabbed hold of him, I can't swim, Rob! The whole time he had known that if they made it through the ship's corridors, that if they got outside through all the panic and the chaos, he would have to jump. Yet he had not shouted, not even once, that he would drown. Was it pride? Had he overlooked it, had he thought he would make it? Without protest he had stepped overboard – jumped wasn't the word. With a certain flourish, actor rehearses jump, next time the cameras roll. "Go, Guus, go." O.K., he had gone. As though jumping off the big table amidst the shards of a wild evening. Of course he had never resurfaced, into the waves and gone. Off the big table, vanished in the shattered glass on the floor. Christ, the whole time knowing that no-one could help him. Jumping hand in hand would have taken both of them into the dark. Clutching at his friend was not an option; he would only try to save him, and thereby drown himself. Had all that gone through his mind as he wrestled his way up from the hold of the *Bungu Maru*? Fighting through the narrow corridors, fighting for their lives. Speed had been everything, the faster, the closer they were to the water. To death, in fact.

"Guus always stood in front of me at roll call – I'll tell you about the ship later. One day a guard knocked him out with one karate chop to the neck. He lay there in the burning sun, no-one looked, no-one was allowed to do anything. I was looking down at him, his head was almost on my foot. It lasted five minutes, no more, but I thought he was dead. Then he opened his eyes, realized what had happened and got up without a sound, perfectly calm, and without drawing any attention to himself, took up his position again. As though no Jap existed, as if there were no camp, no war. At that moment I realized: this is the way to live."

The father was silent.

"He never told me he couldn't swim. Maybe I could have done something if I'd known."

The father looked at him questioningly and leaned back a little to let the waiter set down their coffees. The rattle of the cups, you could imagine a brief earthquake far away in a distant land that had made the cups tremble. But it was only the slight tremor in an old waiter's hand. He told the father about the torpedo attack. And about Bandung, and Thailand, and London, about Java, about all the things Guus had immersed him in. The Guus in him, the Guus he had dreamed up and pursued these last few years. But there was no cohesion to his story. Wreckage from one anecdote cropped up in the next, wisps of memory, loose ends of recollection. He kept apologizing for telling everything so chaotically.

"Did he ever talk about his mother?"

The father's question staggered him. The word "mother"

cut through him. That was *his* word, not even with Guus had he wanted to talk about his mother, deeper than a mineshaft did it go into him. And Guus himself had hardly spoken about his own mother, only his father; he did not know about life with a mother.

"Once, something funny. He said: 'I inherited my mother's grand piano. Even as an angel she's still pulling the strings.'"

It was something, a fragment that stood out now from their chain of conversations on the march from Ban Pong to the first camp. Their iron will to survive that journey, their armoured march, their barricaded world, the look in their eyes, their unshakeable faith in each other's memory. At Bandung they had built up their stockpiles, then lived off them sparingly. "Only when it's gone does it really exist," was their motto. And it *had* gone and it *did* exist, perpetually, and Guus and he met again in the hold of the *Bungu Maru*. Coursing for the Formosa Strait, coursing for the archipelago of a maniac, coursing towards the torpedo, towards the depths. Bang.

"Guus used to sit under the piano for hours while his mother practised. He lived under that piano, he sat there with his toys, he built his playhouse, not in a tree, but under the sounding board. He fell asleep there. And his mother played all she could. She died when Guus was four, before he knew her, really. She was the music, the musical stave in his head."

So that was why Guus had played into the small hours, that was why he had played as the Heinkels opened their bomb bays, that was why he was so elegant and balanced. A stave in his head, a mother who studied on inside him, limping angel, a storehouse of music.

What would Guus have thought about in the waves? His father, his piano, the dogs on the doorstep? Him? When you're dying, you don't think, you are, you *are* to the very last instant. The water around him, gag over his mouth, belt around his breathing, the endless darkness before his eyes. Perhaps he remembered how he had slept under the piano, like a dog in its basket. Perhaps the sounds came back, perhaps he saw his mother's feet on the pedals. Snippets from before the world began, music from before his father, curled up, perfectly silent, sinking, helpless, missing and, finally, gone.

"He talked about you often. Sometimes he worried about how you would make it through the war. He thought the Boche would confiscate De Kolkhof, and that you would be simply put out on the street."

"Guus never left my thoughts, especially when London went up in flames. But I did receive a letter from him, fortunately, via Switzerland. That he was volunteering for the Indies. After that, nothing more, not a word. Only rumours, the war years were full of rumours, half-truths, reports in hindsight. I imagined he had been taken prisoner, I told myself that he was young, an equilibrist, that he would slip free somehow. That's what you hope for, you keep yourself going by painting your own picture of things. It was only after the war that the letter came from Java, reeking of bad news before I had even opened it. Missing. Dead, in other words, although that little fringe of unrest remains. Not being able to visit a grave is hard. Very hard."

Guus' father. The gestures, the timbre, the table between them was slowly stripped and moved away. Guus nestled down in their talk, their words touched, and the silence that arose again and again underscored how close they were. Talking and listening, attention and empathy in tandem. There at the edge of the playground, in a simple café, they made a seaman's grave for a son and a friend. They tossed one wreath after the other. A ring of stories and memories drew close around the dark hole in the ocean, the well in which the ladder only led downwards.

"And you, Rob?"

Inevitable question, impossible question, a gravedigger asking his colleague: so when are *you* going to die?

"What I'd like to know, at least if you want to tell me, of course, is what Guus wrote to you in that last letter. How was he at that moment, was he optimistic, what were his thoughts?"

As though the father had seen the question coming, he pulled an envelope from his inside pocket.

"Why don't you read it?"

He took it, carefully removed the sheets from the envelope, noting the Swiss postmark. "Dear Father ..." The envied father, the close one, the emphatic one. A father like a mother. Not the father he himself had once loved, and once had let go, whose letters he had torn in two and thrown into the sea. "Dear Father," he read. A refined hand, artful little letters, steady, wide margins, space. Light-green ink and no deletions, even though the letter had been written in haste, Guus wrote – someone was going to take it to Switzerland and post it there.

He recognized everything he read. In a few sentences the history of Guus' London months, and his resolute opting for the army and against freedom. Camden, the fire brigade, his hours in Heywood Hill's bookshop. And there it stood: he longed to turn his life towards something else; *aux armes*, to take up arms against the barbarians who had bombed London to rubble and commandeered the Netherlands. Away from the piano stool. "I'm happiest when I'm at my piano, Father, but the music won't come any more. Chopin and Rachmaninov are still brilliant, but I don't dare to play them any more, not while houses around the corner are on fire." Towards the end of the letter, casually: "I'm afraid I never got around to those swimming lessons. But I survived the water from the fire hoses, so I'll just have to take my chances!" And his last words: "I embrace you, Father, give my regards to De Kolkhof and the dogs. Your Guus."

130

He looked up, unable to say a thing, and in truth with no desire to break the silence.

"And you, Rob?"

Could the father not see that he had no answer? What was he supposed to say? That he, like Guus, was going to vanish, go back to South Africa, to the happy hunting grounds, to hell in a handcart?

"I'll be going back soon. To Cape Town, where I live." He did not know what else to say. He lived there, yes. His body sat at the window there and at a table and lay in a bed there. But the end was in sight. He would go back, agreed.

"Shall I show you De Kolkhof? Then we can walk down to the river."

"Do you still live there?"

"No, that was ages ago. The British bombed it, the Germans who were billeted there did not survive. It was our local inferno. The fire brigade arrived too late, on purpose. It's in ruins."

They approached what was left of the house. The coach house was still standing, the pool was a snarl of vines but still discernible, the weeping beech was in blossom as though nothing had ever happened. Again, he recognized it all. Guus' descriptions had been meticulous. The father stopped in his tracks: "That's where the pantry was." Nothing more.

"Do you still have the guns and the rods, and the Voerman and the ..."

"Had to leave it all behind. They came to fetch me one evening, questioned me, wanted to know where Guus was. I could tell them truthfully that, sad to say, I had no idea. They let me go, but the house was requisitioned, I had to find myself somewhere else to live. The British were dropping a lot of bombs around here, Deventer took quite a few hits. I was not allowed to take anything from De Kolkhof, just some photographs and letters, and those only with difficulty. The dogs had to stay as well. Germans liked dogs."

A man with a couple of photographs, a couple of letters. And apparently with no hard feelings, there was no trace of hatred or anger in what he said. He talked about Germans rather than Boche. In sublime equilibrium he seemed to have risen above his sorrow, to have accepted things. Even Guus' death he seemed to have absorbed, or rather, he carried him the way you carry a wounded animal, avoiding every jolt, tenderly, devotedly.

"The river is over there, fifteen minutes. Will you manage?"

Why did he ask if he could walk that far? He himself walked with a cane, what made him suspect Guus' friend might have trouble going the distance? How much did he know?

He nodded, saying little, just looking, remembering Guus' every description. Reconstruction of a paradise. Nothing was the same, but everything was still there, in evaporated form, in drowned words.

"The way the deer's antlers ticked against his handle-bars, its head dangling beside the frame. The subdued triumph, bringing home the kill – my father, the kindest man I know, is a hunter, a good shot. I watched him on many occasion, the way he sat in the twilight with the patience of an ox, waiting for that one buck. Or the way he stood, his gun held up at an angle, turning with the ducks as they passed overhead and saw the birds tumbling down, one, two, sometimes three in a row. The dogs beside him, quivering, panting to hear him say "*apporte*". How he watched them go, called their names and patted their heads contentedly as they laid the ducks at his feet, dripping with water, their eyes fixed on their master. They were soft-mouthed dogs, trained to keep their teeth in check. On the way home my father always hummed; he probably felt like singing, but thought it inappropriate. Then up onto the grounds, past the pool, whatever he had shot we hung in the pantry, then put our bikes in the coach house. And after that he would say: 'Will you play?' No matter if my fingers were stiff with cold, he would sit down beside the piano, his green sweater with the leather sleevelets, his dark-brown hunting trousers, shoes off and his feet on a pile of books. Try forgetting something like that."

Guus. The man who had been out to forget. Or rather, the man who forgot nothing, but was wild about the future, making plans, charting courses, shifting courses if need be. Got to his feet after a chop to the neck, resumed his place in line, ramrod straight, parting down the middle.

He followed the father. The river sparkled in the distance. The thick green grass rolling here and there as in a gentle duneland. It was July, the sun warm and abundantly present. Willows blossomed, small pools of water marked an old break in the dyke. Ducks flew over, he saw swans.

"Here is where Creation began. And not much has changed since. Guus and I came here often."

"Would you mind stopping for a moment? I need to catch my breath."

Guus' father eyed him, was about to say something, but then seemed to think better of it. He pointed to a hillock and stuck his cane into a muddy patch of pasture.

"I'm sorry, I can't make it to the river, my back hurts too much."

Why his back? Why didn't he tell him he was dying, that he was all used up inside, that the pain and the exhaustion had nothing to do with his back? Impossible, he could not possibly tell Guus' father. But he sensed that the man would not be fooled. His silence said enough. He did not ask about his back, did not pursue matters, only stared towards the river, silent as his son's friend.

"I have something for you. One of the few things I

was allowed to take from the house. It's a photograph taken in the last months that Guus studied at home. With a flash. I opened the door without making a sound, and Guus only looked up when he heard the shutter. It's for you."

Guus in his father's room, the room he could have sketched without ever having seen it. He was sitting behind a big desk, bigger than he had imagined. The same kind of desk *he* had sat behind at sixteen, sliding the drawers open and closed searching for nothing, on an ash-grey afternoon, in a lost moment. Brothers out on the ice, mother gone, father present, large as life in a hidden notebook.

He was bent over an unseen problem, a judicial scrimmage, a legal text that had been violated. Flash, shackled motionless, eternally, wall, painting, bookcases, a gun half visible, a corner table with a dried arrangement, a satchel full of papers leaning against the desk. The dream, paradise, the father close by, the future nowhere to be seen. Nowhere, yet the emptiness, the fear, German voices, the bombs that would strike later, the dogs howling during the raid.

He looked towards the river. The yellow sand along its banks stood out brightly. A ship's bell sounded across the pasture. July, the sun at its hottest, the forlornness pervading all. He would have liked to walk into the river, if he could. Run to it, up onto a breakwater, dive. He used to do it with his brothers. Float with the current, climb out two or three breakwaters further down. He was incapable of anything now, even weeping. He put the picture away and struggled to his feet.

On the train trip back he sat for two hours without speaking, people around him smoking, talking. He did not mind, he had never minded strangers. Guus' father had brought him to the station in an old Citroën, identical to the one he had driven in Lourenço Marques. As he was about to board, they had squeezed each other's shoulders. The father made as if to hug him, but he pretended not to notice. He climbed the steps to the dim carriage. The father who watched him go patted him on the back and said: "You made Guus ...", but a hurrying passenger pushed between them, the door swung shut. The driver set the train in motion. Whatever he had meant to say, nothing more was said.

The afternoon was far gone, he stared at the lighted earth, filled with sun, filled with activity. There were a few incoherent thoughts about his mother, and about the days with his brothers after the cremation. Ribbons of landscape sped past his window. But what went on out there no longer reached him. He was yearning for Cape Town.

For tremendous Cape Town.